To me

Enemy Within

Julia C. Hoffman

Julia C. Hoffman

Enemy Within
Copyright ©2015 by Julia C. Hoffman

Cover Design by Chrissy Long
Cover Photo by Julia C. Hoffman

This is a work of fiction. All characters, and events portrayed in these pages are entirely fictional; any resemblance to actual persons, living or dead, is purely coincidental and not intended by the author.

ISBN: 978-0-9963974-3-8

*To the memory of my brother David Cartter (1946-2014),
He answered my questions which gave me the background
and courage to write this book. I am forever grateful.*

Acknowledgements

Thanks to my readers and those that critiqued this book, it is better for your inputs: Sally Owen, David Cartter, Lida Sedaris, and Chris DeSmet, a huge thank-you to Lourdes Venard for her editing and critique, Chrissy Long for her wonderful work on the cover.

I'd like to blame someone for the errors in this book, but sadly they are all mine.

Prologue

✳

It was the kick to the stomach that toppled him. Crying for his mother, he curled into a fetal ball and sought refuge in the earth. His mother didn't come, his cries went unanswered. The earth was silent. The surrounding woods were silent. The kicks increased, faster and wilder. He felt his head being jerked up, but that pain was nothing compared to the pain spreading through his gut. "Your god should have been kicked to the curb a long time ago," he managed to spit out from between clenched teeth. Another kick aimed at his gut made him try to claw open the ground and crawl in. "Can't stand the truth," he managed to force out. The kicks became stomps.

"There is no god but God," a man screamed from the depths of madness. "And your god listens to the whispers of Satan," said the man on the ground. The next kick shattered his teeth. "So you know what I say is true," he spit out, and his shattered teeth followed.

The blows continued. He closed his eyes and let the world spin around him.

He woke alone and watched as the heavens circled the pole star. "God," he whispered, "can you hear me? Do not let me die here. Do not let me die alone."

Inch by inch he pulled himself uphill across the dirt, twigs, brush, and the scarlet leaves of autumn. Once he rolled down the incline, causing him to clench his jaw, which loosened what teeth remained. He spit them out and started again. The going got tough.

He lost his grip on the dirt and finally could not move. The cold surged up through his legs to his back. With what strength he had left, he rolled onto his back and looked up. The moon and the stars shone upon him as he lost his place in this world.

1

✳

It was a blessing. The baby finally slept. With the movement of the car, the warmth of the sun and Phil's hand in hers, Edie Swift took the opportunity to catch up on her sleep.

Phil looked over at the sleeping Edie for a moment, even in sleep she was dynamic. Their friends always said that they could feel Edie before they saw her. He tucked a few strands of her auburn hair that escaped from her ever present ponytail behind her ear, then placed his hand around her's. And wondered again how they ever lasted long enough to have a baby. No one else ever thought they would, especially after hearing about Edie arresting Phil for drunk driving, property damage, resisting arrest. (Most women thought the D.A. should have added charges for the worst pick-up line ever. And worst delivery time—during an arrest.) But there the baby was, secure and asleep in the back seat. Who'd a thunk that would ever happen? Not Phil.

Phil Best enjoyed this quiet drive down Wisconsin Highway 19. His days were filled with employees' troubles, and his nights were now filled with a baby crying at midnight and other odd hours. This drive was serene.

The reds and golds of the Wisconsin autumn, accentuated by a deep blue sky, triggered a deep yearning in him; to once again be on a Sunday drive with his parents and squabbling sisters, with his nose pressed against the car window as towns gave way to farms where fields stopped at the forest's edge. He wanted to be enveloped by the splendor of autumn. Most of all, he wanted his father's sure hand to be guiding the car. But those times were no more. So Phil kept his eyes on the road, yawned, and when Edie's hand slipped from his, he rolled down his car window to catch what breeze there was and started to hum—anything to keep himself awake.

He made a left–hand turn into Indian Lake Park. The picnic shelter looked empty. At the far end of the park, just beyond the lake, a truck, towing a john-boat, was pulling onto the highway. Our lucky day, Phil thought, we'll have the park to ourselves. No, damn it, he was wrong, there was a car in the parking lot. Maybe those people would leave soon. Phil could only hope. He pulled into the spot next to the parked car.

Edie jolted awake. "Get us out of here. Now," she commanded.

"Quiet," whispered Phil, "you'll wake the baby."

"Turn the car around and get us out of here," Edie demanded again as she scanned the park: only one other car in the parking lot, no one, that she could see, was in the park.

"No," Phil said. "I didn't come all this way for nothing. We came to hike Indian Lake. That's what we are going to do." He got out of the car and went around it to open Edie's door. "Let's go."

"Don't you stubborn Germans ever listen to anyone? I said to get out of here," Edie said, pulling the door back.

"Look who's calling the kettle black. You wanted to come here to hike . . . so we're going to hike."

"I've changed my mind."

"Why?"

Edie paused, would he believe her?

"So, you have no good reason," said Phil.

"Death is here."

"What are you talking about? How do you know that? I didn't see any signs announcing that when I drove in."

"Didn't you feel it?"

"I felt sunshine. I felt a cool breeze. I felt relief that you and Hillary were asleep. I felt nothing else. Tell me, what does death feel like?"

"You didn't feel . . . ?"

Screams rolling down the hill interrupted her. Edie and Phil suspended their argument and turned as a unit toward the shock wave of sounds. Edie shoved the car door open, causing Phil to stumble back against the car and slide to the pavement. Edie ran toward the hill as if pulled by the screams.

"Don't, Edie," Phil yelled, picking himself off the ground. "You're on leave. Remember the baby. Call for help." He yelled anything to get her to stop. But nothing could stop her. Nothing did.

"Can't call, don't know what I have. You watch the baby," Edie yelled back as she ran.

The screams bounced among the trees and brush, announcing the two girls before they ran into Edie's arms.

Edie guided the sobbing girls back to the car, placed them in the front seat, and wrapped a blanket, retrieved from the trunk, around them. It helped. Though the tears continued, the girls stopped shaking, and their cries lessened.

"My name's Edie, I'm with the sheriff's department. This is my husband, Phil." Why the hell did she say that? They weren't married. How many times had he proposed and she said no? Did she want to protect him against ungoverned teenage hormones? Calm the girls? What the hell, that isn't going to happen again, thought Edie. "What happened?" she asked the girls.

Through their sobs, Edie pieced together that there was something on the hill. At the top of the hill. Near the chapel. It was bloody. It was awful.

Phil looked at Edie; she had dropped into detective mode. Their perfect day was cancelled.

He leaned toward her. "Was that a proposal?" he whispered in Edie's ear.

She elbowed him in the ribs. Those elbows were sharp. Phil gently rubbed the area to make sure his ribs were still intact.

Edie saw the exasperated look on Phil's face, shrugged her shoulders. "You know how important my work is to me."

It was a reminder, again, how much Edie could surmise from a smile, a frown, averted eyes, or the silences between words. The last six weeks since the birth of their baby seemed to have pushed the job and everything else, except him, from her mind. The baby consumed her days and nights.

"I thought a baby might change that," said Phil.

"What? You thought I'd become your little woman just because I had a baby? What's that German saying, *kinder, kirche,* and what?"

"*Kinder, küche, kirche.* It was fine for my parents, my grandparents, my great-grandparents, and my great-great—"

"It's not fine for me. Do some time travel, fast. We are in the twenty-first century. I and lots of women have talents and interests beyond the home. I didn't think I needed to point out that Hillary has two parents to guide her, not one. You're *it*." Edie heard some mewing from the back seat; she bent down to see if Hillary was awake.

"Is that a baby?" asked one of the girls between sobs.

"Yes," replied Edie.

"Can we hold him?"

"This baby is a she, and yes," said Edie as she unbuckled Hillary and settled her in the arms of one of the girls. "Support her head and neck." The girls pulled the blanket over their heads and began cooing. With the baby in theirs arms, their cries and tears subsided.

Across the car hood, Edie stared at Phil. "Call 9-1-1, and then Gracie. If you need me, call. Watch those girls closely, they've got my baby," she said and took off running toward the hill.

"Edie, come back, you're not on duty. Wait till someone gets here. Is your phone turned on? Do you even have your phone?" He was wasting his breath. All he could do now was watch the love of his life run toward a collision with trouble and possibly death. *Damn, why couldn't this have stayed a man's world where the little woman was kept in the kitchen, barefoot and pregnant?* Phil laughed as an image of Edie surrounded by a multitude of their children clinging to her apron popped into his head. Edie would never be that woman. She could never be content as an earth mother; she needed space, she needed to fly. He had been warned about her by his mother but there was something about Edith Swift that drew him to her. So Phil stood his ground and watched until the woods enveloped her, hoping that his vigilance would be enough to protect her.

When Edie finally disappeared into the trees and brush, he turned back to his baby and the two girls hidden beneath a blanket. "What am I going to do with three crying girls?" he mumbled to himself as he pulled his cell from his pocket and punched in 9-1-1 and gave them what sketchy details he knew, and then made the call to Gracie. While he waited for the deluge of cops, Phil, once again, looked at his phone; he needed an upgrade so he would have something to do as he waited for Edie.

"Damn," said Edie, slowing to a walk. "Haven't worked out for six weeks and this hill is kicking my butt. I start getting back in shape tonight."

Echoes of the girls' screams seemed to be rebounding through the woods. Edie picked up her pace. Nearing the top of the hill, her police training took over. She slowed to a walk. *Was anything out of place?* Hard to tell with the trees shedding their leaves, she thought. *Any footprints?* Only two sets, presumably made by the girls. *Any broken branches, twigs?* None that she could see. *Anyone on the hill?* Not in plain sight. The scent of a campfire lingered among the trees. *Who had burned what and where?*

As Edie crested the hill, she heard sirens, lots of them. *Must be a slow day,* she thought as she continued to carefully work her way along the leaf strewn path. She could see where the girls had stopped. She skirted their footprints, looked up, and then stopped exactly where the girls had stopped. She saw why the girls screamed. Edie suppressed her screams. Experienced as she was in the gore of police work, this scene took her by surprise. Edie took deep breaths, letting each out slowly. At last her body released a shudder, and she could move.

Something bloody had crawled out of the woods, and it was in front of her. Not moving. Edie surveyed the ground. There were no footprints beyond where she stood. No broken brush except where that bloody, possibly human, thing had crawled. Edie followed the short bloody dirt path to the chapel, St. Mary of the Oaks, built by farmer John Endres in thanks that his prayers were answered and his family saved. She squatted down beside the bloody wreck of what was once a man. *Sad, this man could have used Endres' prayers.* The musty scent of decaying leaves mingled with the pungent stench of dirt soaked in blood was an intense odor that hit her nose. Edie controlled her desire to vomit, and did not turn away. It was obvious he was dead, but still she searched for a carotid pulse that she knew would not be there.

Edie ignored the pain in her quads as she settled into a squat and talked to the remnants of a man who would never again answer anyone. "Who are you? Where did you come from? Was this a crime of opportunity or by design? Why here? Why now? Why you? Did this happen because you were a black man? What can you tell me to help me find the person who did this? And once upon a time, whose little one were you?" Edie looked at the body as if it would easily give up its clues, but they never had, and they never would.

A twig snapped. Edie kept her head down as she slowly turned to the sound. She stood up, turning into two Glocks pointed at her.

"Keep your hands where we can see them," demanded one of the deputies.

"Put those guns down, you crackers," came the command from behind the deputies. "That's Edie Swift. She's one of us." There was only one voice like that, Lieutenant Gracie Davis. It was common knowledge inside the Dane County Sheriff's Department, and out of it, that you obeyed Lieutenant Grace Davis or kissed your ass good-bye. The deputies lowered their guns. One deputy, after viewing the body, stepped to the side of the trail and puked.

"Thanks, Gracie," said Edie to the six-foot-tall black woman.

"What do we have here?" Gracie Davis asked, while throwing Edie a small bottle of hand sanitizer.

"A dead man. Why do you carry this stuff?" asked Edie, after squeezing some onto her palm.

"Habit. Carried it when my kids were little and find it still handy to keep one around. Why don't you?"

"Just became a mother, didn't know I was required to carry the stuff."

"You should start. It's never too early or late to establish a good habit."

"Why didn't you call for an ambulance?" interrupted one of the deputies.

Lieutenant Davis scowled at him. The deputy didn't get the message.

"Because he is dead," replied Edie, thinking, so are you, if you don't shut up.

"How did you know?" the deputy continued to demand.

"I know a dead man when I see one." She had seen many, and remembered each of the dead, in detail, that she had been called to investigate.

Gracie had enough of the I-have-a-penis-and-you-don't game and sent both deputies down the hill to close off the park and direct the crime scene personnel to the top of the hill and send the ambulance back to its base. What they needed was the medical examiner, not paramedics.

"You got here fast," said Edie, after the puking deputy and his partner left.

"Heard the call. As soon as Phil's name came over the scanner, I was out the door. Knew there was trouble.

And that you'd be in the thick of it. His call to me confirmed it," said Gracie. "Tell me, again, what you saw."

"I saw nothing. One car, other than ours, in the parking lot. I didn't see anyone in or near the park until the two girls, who are now sitting in my car, came screaming off the hill. Only footprints here are mine and the girls. You can see where they stopped and where I walked around them and the dead man."

"Did you ID him?"

"No. I'm not carrying any protective equipment, and I wasn't going to touch him beyond looking for a carotid pulse."

"Why don't you have equipment with you?"

"This may come as a shock to you, but I'm on maternity leave. Remember? This started out as a family outing; I wasn't expecting to do police business."

"Doesn't matter, you should be prepared. You should at least have a first aid kit in your car. Once a cop, always a cop—you know that," Gracie said. "What did you say you were doing here?"

"Phil and I planned a hike."

Gracie shook her head, not quite believing Edie. "Can't picture you out for a leisurely stroll, even with Phil and that new baby along. You are not the most relaxing person I know. You and trouble always seem to find each other." Gracie studied the scene. "Gone any farther than this?"

"No. And it was a hike, not a stroll."

"Good," said Gracie ignoring Edie's corrections. "When the crime scene team gets here, we'll go exploring. Here, take this," said Gracie, handing her coat to Edie.

"I'm not cold."

"You're leaking."

Edie looked down at her shirt; the wet streaks started at each nipple and pooled at the hem of her shirt. "The parenting books never mention this stuff," muttered Edie. "I'll go feed Hillary and come back."

"No need to," said Phil, picking his way along the trail with Hillary cocooned in his arms.

"Who let you up?" demanded Gracie.

"They all did. Seems that crying babies make them nervous. I didn't know cops were a bunch of pansies."

"Don't let the baby see this," Edie insisted.

"Why not?" asked Phil.

"Who knows how, or if, this will be imprinted on her memory," replied Edie.

"But she's just a baby," insisted Phil.

"Don't argue with the kid's mother. Do as she asks," said Gracie.

"But—" said Phil.

"But nothing. When that child is older, she'll do all the arguing with Edie for you," said Gracie. "Right now that baby is hungry and we'd all appreciate her being fed. Give Edie the baby."

Phil shut up. He had learned not to argue with Gracie. He waited as Edie searched for a place to sit so she could nurse Hillary.

Edie ignored the bench at the far edge of the clearing, she wanted to see and hear what was happening. She stepped off the path, sat against an oak tree, and found a sweet spot to lean against; she took Hillary from Phil and guided the baby toward a nipple.

The deputies returned with equipment and the crime scene investigators. As they walked past, they turned their heads away from the mother and child.

"Never seen boobs!" Edie yelled after them.

"Not on one of their own," Gracie replied for them.

"What's she doing here?" demanded Sadie Carpenter, looking for a place to set her equipment. "Isn't she on maternity leave?"

"She stays. She was first on scene. I want her eyes on this," said Gracie.

"Leave her alone," said Ben Harris, pushing past Sadie. "You can bitch–slap her later."

"I could take her, easily," said Sadie, following Ben.

"That would be a first. Tell me when and where this bout will be; I'll make a fortune selling tickets."

"Quit the chatter and do your work," commanded Gracie. "I want the detectives on this fast."

Sadie Carpenter pulled out her camera. "They probably contaminated the scene," she shouted to Ben, who was standing next to her.

"The footprints near the body are mine," Edie shouted back. "The only body part I touched was the carotid."

Edie took Hillary off the breast and handed her back to Phil. "There's another blanket in the diaper bag. Put this one in the trunk, I'll wash it this evening."

"How long is this going to take?" asked Phil, as he wrapped his jacket around his baby and stuffed the other blanket in his back pocket.

Edie looked at Gracie, who shrugged her shoulders in reply. "Should be done by the next feeding. You got some place you want to be?" said Edie.

"No. Couldn't go anyway, the deputies won't let me leave. And I'm trying to avoid the press, who are here in force. Don't need Hillary's fifteen minutes of fame to be at a crime scene."

"Did they see her?"

"Yes."

"Any pictures taken?

"Don't know."

"Damn," said Edie. "I can see tonight's headline: 'Baby found at murder scene'. Sensationalism hasn't gone out of style. Hope they don't know she's mine."

"I'll do what I can to guide them in a different story direction," said Gracie. "But if it's a slow news day, you know what'll happen."

"Think whoever did this is still here?" asked Phil, looking around the crime scene—his first.

"Can't tell. Probably not. Ready, Edie?" said Gracie.

Edie nodded. Then stood to watch as Phil settled Hillary into the crook of his arm and followed a deputy down the hill. "Don't let them take pictures of Hillary," Edie shouted after them. She stood and watched until Phil and their baby were out of sight, then turned to Lieutenant Davis. "Let's go."

2

✳

The dead man's trail was easy to follow. Blood and the crushed undergrowth detailed his climb. From the safety of the maples and oaks, blue jays squawked at the intrusion of Gracie, Edie, Ben, and the uniformed deputies. Two white–tailed deer were scared up as the group went past. The bloody path seemed to go on forever. At the end of the trail, the woods opened, and then closed again yards beyond the blood-splattered trail they had been following. In the opening were the charred remains of a campfire, and dirt that had been ground to dust; in other places were clods of dirt formed by congealed blood. Lots of blood. *It was a miracle,* thought Edie, *that the dead man made it to the top of the hill. With the trees rapidly shedding their leaves, and winter following, he probably wouldn't have been found till next year.*

"Look at all that blood," said Gracie. "What an ugly way to die."

"Is there a good way to die?" Edie asked.

"In my bed, and in my sleep, and quietly. That's my plan," replied Gracie.

"I had a cousin die while hunting," said one of the deputies. "He loved hunting."

"One of my cousins died in a snowmobile accident," said Ben Harris, as he focused his camera for another shot.

The group waited for the story.

"Aren't you going to tell us the rest of the story?" Gracie demanded.

Ben stopped shooting the area. "What were we discussing?"

"Your cousin's death," said Edie.

"Which cousin?" Ben asked.

"The snowmobile death," said Gracie.

"Oh, that one."

"You got more than one unusual death in your family to tell us about?" Gracie asked.

"Yeah, but this cousin was extra stupid, he went out snowmobiling alone at night, on a lake, with heavy ground fog and he drove into open water," said Ben, returning to his photos. "Stupid, just stupid. It was rumored that a cousin created a Darwin Award certificate for him and placed it in the coffin."

"That's mean. The guy was probably just drunk," said Edie.

"That too, stupid and drunk. Deadly combination," said Ben as he went back to his shooting.

"What about you, Edie, you got any odd family death stories?" Gracie asked.

"War, accidents, the usual causes of death. Let's get back to this case," said Edie, trying to bring the focus back to the dead man. "How'd he ever make it to the chapel?"

"Everyone stay put till I get my photos," said Ben, taking close-ups of the scene. "More than one person was here."

"That's obvious. What else can you tell us?" asked Gracie.

"At this time . . . more than one person was here."

"I can see that. I want to know who besides the dead man was here. Have they left any traces besides indistinct footprints in the dust? Let us know when you're done; I'd like to explore some more," said Gracie. "The rest of you, without moving from where you are, look around. Do you see anything?"

"Can't see anything from here," said Edie as she did a three-hundred-sixty degree turn.

"We'll check the perimeter. You," Gracie said, pointing at one of the uniformed deputies, "what's your name?"

"I'm Smith, ma'am."

"Deputy Smith, you come with me. And . . . what's your name?"

"Johnson, ma'am."

"You stay with this group."

Lieutenant Gracie Davis and Deputy Smith searched the perimeter of the stomping ground. The path was easy to find, the brush was trampled. "Amateurs, they're making this part of the job easy," said Gracie. "Found a path," she yelled back, "Edie, you need to be here."

"Stay off from it," yelled Ben. "I'll be finished here in a few moments."

Edie took another look around. Soon it would be relinquished to the scene investigators to go over inch by inch. With a scene this large, who knew how long it would be before she could scour the site herself. Edie stopped herself, she was on maternity leave, and this crime would be someone else's problem to solve. She joined Gracie and Smith.

Gracie Davis didn't like to be told what to do. And she didn't like to wait. She hadn't climbed the career ladder to be told by anyone to wait. "I'll stay off to the side."

"No. You will stay put. Edie, that goes for you, too."

Gracie stayed put, but not still; she rocked back and forth, rising on her toes and settling back on her heels, twisting from side to side, turning three-hundred-sixty degrees in an attempt to look everywhere at once. She was rooted to one spot, but she wasn't passive. Edie matched Gracie's moves; it was as if they were performing a well-known ballet.

Edie heard a chuckle from Ben between camera clicks. "What's funny?"

"You two."

Edie looked at Gracie; she didn't see anything funny, just a cop anxious to get on with her job. She looked at the mud made of dirt and blood. "I don't see anything funny."

"You have to be here," said Ben.

Finally, Ben Harris stood at Gracie's side and led the way, snapping photos, as they went into the woods. When the path forked, the group stopped.

"Ben, it's your call. Which way?" said Gracie.

"We'll follow the path to the left," Ben replied.

"I'll take the right," said Edie.

"No, you will stay with the group. We can check the other side when we come back."

Smith pulled his Glock.

"Holster that gun. There's only us and the deer in these woods. And it ain't hunting season yet," commanded Gracie.

Smith took his time putting his gun in the holster, but kept his hand on his Glock as he followed Edie, Ben Harris, and Lieutenant Davis into the woods. At the end of the path, the group found a dirt road, a field of corn stubble, and the beginning of the other path.

"Looks like this was their way in. Why isn't this entrance sealed off? Smith, go stand near the highway. No one is to come in or go out. I'll send Johnson to assist when we get back to the parking lot," directed Lieutenant Davis.

Smith yanked out his gun, turning off the safety, as he walked to his new post.

Edie watched Smith pick his way along the field road; the itch to push the case forward surfaced. Edie sighed. She couldn't scratch that itch. Damn.

"What are you thinking?" Edie asked Gracie as they returned to the stomping ground.

"That we should've closed that part of the park earlier."

"I meant about the case," said Edie.

"I'm seeing the tramplings of a herd of elephants," said Gracie.

"So," said Edie, "they want us to catch them, or we weren't supposed to notice because whoever did this thought he was dead and would stay put and the body wouldn't be discovered for a long time, or they're inexperienced or the weather didn't cooperate by making this place mud."

"Or all of the above," said Gracie.

"When can I get a closer look at the scene?" Edie asked.

"After the crime scene people are done, you know that. Take a good look now, this maybe what you get for a while," said Gracie with a smile.

"They'll have trampled over all the evidence," Edie said loud enough for Ben to hear.

"At least we'll have evidence," Ben shouted back.

The body was bagged when Edie, Gracie, and Johnson got back to the chapel. A deputy handed Lieutenant Davis the dead man's identification.

"Dumb criminals," Gracie said shuffling through the IDs before handing them to Edie.

Edie let out a low whistle as she shuffled through the contents taken from the dead man's wallet. Russell Washington, Atlanta, Georgia, looked back from the driver's license. His FBI card was right behind it. "Mr. Washington, you came a long way to die. Whoever did this just went from dumb to dumber. Looks like they've earned themselves a collective Darwin Award," she said, handing the IDs back to Gracie. "He's got a key for that newest boutique hotel downtown—The Morning Rose."

"Better give them a call. Talk with the manager, tell them not to disturb the room," Lieutenant Davis said to Edie.

"Can I use your phone?"

"What's wrong with yours?"

"Since I'm on maternity leave, my work phone is back in the office."

Gracie Davis handed her phone to Edie. "And why aren't you carrying your personal phone?"

"'Cause I was with Phil. And who do you think you are?"

"Your boss and a friend. You should know that life is a little easier if you stay connected."

"When I'm working, I carry a phone. When I'm not working I like to see what's around me, not glued to a smartphone screen."

"They come in handy."

"And so do I."

"You're life isn't just about you anymore, you've got a little one."

"And when I'm not with her, she has another parent."

"It's different."

"Prove it," said Edie.

Walking down the hill with Gracie, Edie saw that the parking lot was full. She counted three TV news trucks, the medical examiner's vehicle, Phil's car, the girls' car, multiple squad cars, her friend and reporter Mark Uselman's car, and a few vehicles she could not place.

"I think you should cut your maternity leave short," said Gracie as they made their way to the flats.

"Why?"

"You're already deep into this case. Might as well get paid for it."

"I've got eight more weeks of maternity leave. Let someone else handle this."

"I'd like you to."

"It'll cost you."

"How much?"

"The last eight weeks of my leave and more. When this is done, I go back on maternity leave with comp time added. I work only this case. And I determine which hours I work."

"I'll get back to you. Got time to write up a report on this incident?"

"Between feedings and my naps . . . maybe."

The women stopped at the bottom of the hill. They saw the flimsy crime scene tape and the reporters beyond waiting for a story. When the reporters saw them, a race to the police tape began; at the flimsy tape they stopped and jockeyed to be in position to get their questions answered first.

Their questions changed when they recognized Edie. The old–timers of the press corps had been known to point the newbies toward Edie Swift. Follow her around, the cub reporters were told; she was always good for a story. She never disappointed and here she was at a crime scene. It was a good day for them.

"Edie, Edie, over here!" shouted Morris Brennan. "What are you doing here? Thought you had a baby. Say, is that your baby over there?"

"Yeah," she replied, ducking under the crime scene tape.

"Give us an interview," demanded Leigh Stone, the newest Madison reporter.

"I'm on maternity leave; Lieutenant Gracie Davis will answer your questions."

"My experience says that where you are, there's always a good story. How about giving it to us?" said Mark Uselman.

"Sorry, Mark, I'm just a civilian today. Talk to Lieutenant Davis."

"Don't buy it," said Tim O'Malley. "You've got a nose for trouble. Answer a few questions. What happened here?"

"If you're a civilian, what were you doing here?" Leigh Stone demanded.

That stopped Edie. Edie turned, sized up the new reporter, and then turned again and kept on walking—she wasn't worth it.

"It's your civic responsibility to answer questions!" Leigh Stone shouted.

Edie's back stiffened, but she kept on walking.

"Shut up," Mark Uselman cautioned Stone.

"You shut up, I'm trying to get a story," said Leigh.

"Keep it up, you might get a fist in your face," said Morris Brennan, joining his fellow reporters.

Leigh Stone ignored their advice. "Can I get a picture with you and your baby?"

Edie, who had opened her car door, turned and in what seemed a few seconds was back at the cluster of reporters, planting her face in Leigh Stone's face.

Leigh Stone took a few steps back.

Edie Swift followed. "No. Not today. Not ever. You were informed that Lieutenant Davis would be answering your questions. Today I am a civilian. You do not have permission to use any pictures you took of me and certainly none that you may have taken of my family. You continue this harassment, the next voice your station manager will hear is my lawyer's."

Edie watched as Leigh Stone almost dropped her mike and took a giant step back away from her.

Edie returned to her car.

Lieutenant Gracie Davis smiled as she watched the confrontation. She had Edie Swift right where she wanted her—back on her team.

"Told you so," said Morris, after he saw Edie get into the car. "Don't try to push Edie Swift around. It's never worked."

"I'll find a way," said Leigh.

"Is that a bet?" Morris asked.

"We all heard it, Leigh," said Tim O'Malley. "What's the bet and what's the time frame?"

"The wrap on this story," said Leigh.

"Dinner for all of us at The Ovens," said Tim.

"With dessert," said Morris.

"And drinks, before, during and after the meal," Mark added.

The roasting of Leigh Stone was interrupted by a scanner requesting assistance at the Victor Berger High School to control student fighting.

"Sounds like a big one," said Morris Brennan to his cameraman. "We'll get in a few questions here, then head for the school."

Leigh Stone pushed past the other reporters to question Lieutenant Davis.

Edie settled into the front seat as Phil buckled Hillary into her car seat.

"The vultures done?" asked Phil.

"They're just doing their job," said Edie.

"Poking their noses into other people's business?"

"Sometimes. This one may be big. The dead man was with the FBI."

"That was an ugly scene," Phil said as he slid into the driver's seat.

"They're all ugly. You can't tell anyone about today."

"Don't you trust me not to tell?"

"I do, but I need to give a disclaimer every time," said Edie, buying time to figure out how to break the news of another twist in their lives. "Gracie wants me on this case."

"Why? You've got another eight weeks of leave! Why you?"

"Because I'm good at what I do, and I was first on the scene."

"What does that mean for us? Do you really want to go back early?"

"Maybe, if Gracie can honor my requests. I asked to be assigned only to this case, that I decide my hours and a resumption of my leave when this case is over."

"I know what you're going to do, you'll go back early. And you'll stay back. I want you to promise that you'll resume your leave after this case."

"If I take this case, yes, I can promise that. But if I go back, I don't understand why I shouldn't stay on the job."

"Hillary. And I need more assurance than that. I want something better."

"What could be better than my word?"

Phil looked at Edie, and then down at his hands. "Swear on Hillary's life."

"No. I'm not putting her in harm's way—ever."

"Then you admit you're going back."

"For this case only."

No good oaths for Edie to swear to popped into Phil's head. "Okay, do a pinkie swear."

"What is a pinkie swear?"

"Do I look like a girl? I don't know, thought you might."

"Never done one. Maybe you should ask one of your sisters."

"That's where I heard it. I think they made me cross pinkie fingers with them, and then swear to something.

"Okay."

Edie and Phil crossed pinkies while Edie said, "I swear that I will only work on this case and return to my leave when it is over, or I hope to die."

"Don't swear to that, I'm not good with midnight feedings."

Edie pulled out her phone and punched in Brooke Rivera's number.

"Who you calling?"

"Brooke Rivera. Leigh Stone, that new TV reporter, suggested she was going to publish photos of you and Hillary. I suggested that Brooke would have a talk with Leigh's manager. Just following through."

3

✳

Edie sat at her kitchen table counting the diapers on the clothesline. "How can one so little go through so many diapers in a day?" she said to herself. "Never thought my life would turn into one long butt wipe." She laughed at herself. "Better than butt kissing." She looked down at the blank pad of paper and did not know where to begin with the report for Lieutenant Davis. Only six weeks since Hillary's birth and she was out of shape physically and mentally flabby. Enough. She grabbed the baby monitor, took it to Phil in the living room, "Here, you listen for Hillary. I'm starting my run."

"Got your cell? I may need you."

"You won't, fed her thirty minutes ago, and then put a clean diaper on her. Now she's asleep, which would be a good time for me to go on a run and for you to pick up this mess."

"But—"

"But nothing, it's time to gain some control of our lives. And, yes, I do have my cell."

"Is it on?"

Edie flipped open the phone, turned it on, and then showed it to Phil. "Yes."

"Just checking. See you later. Take a flashlight, these farmers aren't watching for you. They don't expect anyone is crazy enough to be jogging on their roads at this time of day . . . or year. Or really anytime."

Edie ignored him and stepped into the night.

For a moment, Edie stood on the front step deciding which way to run. North would take her into farm country on roads busy with combines, tractors, and semis trying to bring in the harvest before rain or frost settled on the crops or worse than that, snow that came and didn't melt until April.

South would take her into Troutbeck, where the few sidewalks it had were rolled up at six p.m., but there wasn't any farm traffic in the burg. South, into the village, it was. A slight odor of diesel fumes, probably from Phil's trucking business that held down one corner of Troutbeck, hung in the air, mingled with the scent of burning autumn leaves.

Edie jogged past a road sign announcing Troutbeck, unincorporated. She still couldn't believe that she had agreed to move from Madison to Troutbeck. What was Troutbeck compared to her Madison?

Fellow deputies, when they heard she was moving to Troutbeck, warned her about the town; their best advice was not to move there. But—if she really had to—slow down.

Edie remembered the day the self-appointed Troutbeck historian and greeter to the community had clued her into the simmering controversies of the town. And told her and Phil to be careful; sometimes the controversies broke to the surface, ending in fistfights. Phil suddenly remembered work he had to do in the shop. Edie was left alone with the historian. Edie left the dishes unpacked in the moving boxes, put on her poker face, and listened to the historian.

It was a well–known fact, the historian told Edie, that the government used this peaceful burg as a revenue source. Every Friday and Saturday night they handed out speeding tickets right and left to the patrons of Lower Bottom, who for some reason forget the speed limit signs and raced past the church into the arms of deputies ready with radar guns and speeding tickets.

Another faction, the historian went on to enumerate, states that the Troutbeck minister and the cops are in cahoots. That the minister had talked the cops into setting up speed traps every Friday and Saturday night. As long as his pews were filled on Sunday, the cops could keep the money.

And this last theory just might hold water, the historian continued, as on Sunday the patrons of Lower Bottom's strip clubs and booze bars (and, he added in a whisper, probably other nefarious goings-on) would be sitting in the pews next to their fuming wives. And the collection plates would overflow with money from the penitents who reached deep into their pockets under the intense stares of their wives and Mr. Acker, whose eyes bored into theirs with a shit-eating grin plastered on his face. Mr. Acker's house was at the edge of the village, a few yards where the deputies stopped the speeders coming from Lower Bottom. He saw one transgression and guessed at the other one.

And, yet, there was another faction that, the rumor was, didn't really care. The historian could hardly believe this one. Did it really matter why Troutbeck was a speed trap, they wondered. Did it really matter that Lower Bottom's strip clubs were filled? And this faction went on to damn the police for catching speeders. And they would go on to damn the people who built the church and took away what little joy they had.

But, the historian concluded, every Friday and Saturday night Lower Bottom was full. And the police waited on the outskirts of Troutbeck to hand out tickets. And every Sunday the Troutbeck church was filled. And its coffers overflowed.

It was a conundrum and very divisive, said the historian, and then left.

Leaving Edie to wonder why she left Madison.

On her first jog through Troutbeck, Edie took a closer look at the village. To her it looked like a bump in a country road. A random place where two roads intersected and people built some houses, like many places in Wisconsin. But, according to what she could glean from the historian's lecture, she was misinformed.

Edie jogged past Mrs. Voss's and the VandenHuevel's making a mental note to introduce herself; she had been told they had a daughter who might babysit. She continued past the empty store on the corner.

Edie turned east away from the dark roads into the village where there were a few streetlights; she didn't want to be someone's roadkill. She noted the lights were on in the church, and lots of cars were parked out front. Edie ran the other way. She wanted to avoid anyone coming out of the church. She knew that someone would stop her and innocently inquire about the dead man. Somehow they all knew who she was and what her job was and, though each person wanted to know her, they wanted to know the inside story more.

Her route took her past the scary house, the one that did more than put carved pumpkins on the front steps for Halloween. Those people enjoyed Halloween and displayed their enthusiasm. A skeleton hung from the tree. A fenced-in graveyard erected in the front yard which, Carole Rhyme, Edie's first friend from Troutbeck, said seemed to get bigger every year. Spiderwebs covered the porch with huge spiders off to one side, waiting for the next prey. A statue of Dracula opening a coffin lid was the focus of the ground display. Ghosts flew from the trees. A witch on a broomstick hovered near the roof. For Edie, this was over the top. Gory stuff was part of Edie's job, but she didn't like to be reminded of it in her neighborhood. Edie quickened her pace as she approached the Halloween house.

She turned right at the corner and ran down one of the two streets in town. Then she ran up the street, and then down it, again, and then ran on the other street in town, and then back again. This was boring. Please let the harvest be done–soon, she begged.

After twenty minutes of jogging the few streets of Troutbeck, she noticed her friend Carole Rhyme sitting on the porch sipping from a cup.

"Looking good, almost makes me wish I was a masochist like you," Carole called out. "Do one lap for me."

"Join me, you'd lose some of your aggressive tendencies," said Edie, running in place as she talked to Carole.

"I can do that brushing my clients' hair."

"I've noticed. What you drinking?"

"My winter special, Bailey's and hot chocolate."

"It isn't winter."

"It's close enough. Can't stand any more of Ray's brew concoctions. His pumpkin beer is atrocious this year. Want one of my specials?"

"Of course."

"A drinking mom. What will the world think?"

"One drink in almost eleven months is not going to hurt me or Hillary."

"Come on up, I've got yours right here," Carole said. She scooted over to make room for Edie, handed her a cup of hot chocolate with a splash of Bailey's Irish Cream. "Did you run past the Halloween house?"

"You can't miss it. I sprinted past it. It gives me the creeps."

"Me, too. Why do they need a graveyard in their front yard when one is almost in their backyard? Just don't understand it; they're nice people, though. Have you met them yet?"

"No."

"She's one of my clients. Remind me to introduce you two. Saw you on TV. What's the scoop?"

"Dead man found at Indian Lake."

"Not giving anything out."

"Can't. Need to notify next of kin and all that. But more than that, once you say something, it can never be retrieved."

"Don't trust me? I keep lots of secrets, I'm a hair-dresser."

"Didn't know that stylists had provider–client privileges."

"They sure do. How do you think I keep my clients?

"You're a good stylist."

"True, but they trust me with more than their hair. I keep their secrets. Once I start shampooing and giving a head message, my clients relax and start blabbing. They know that what goes in my ears does not come out my mouth. Seeing your hair, when was the last time you were in?"

"Before Hillary was born."

"Too long. Come into the studio. I'll do it now."

"I didn't bring any money."

"Pay me tomorrow. I trust you."

Edie followed Carole to the back of her house where her salon was, set her cup of hot chocolate down and as Carole washed her hair, relaxed.

"See, what did I tell you? This is one of the most relaxing things in the world. Got anything you want to tell me?"

"No."

Carole rinsed Edie's hair, and then sat her up. "You're tensing up again," said Carole combing Edie's hair.

"Gotta make a decision, continue my leave or go back to work."

"Working on the dead man's case?"

"Yeah. My lieutenant would like me on the case, Phil doesn't . . . and I'm divided."

"Hillary?"

"I thought parenthood would be easier."

"Every beginner parent does. Which way are you leaning?"

"I'm not. I'm on the fence."

"If you decide to go back, you can leave Hillary with me."

"You have your own work."

"Which I did while raising my kids. And with a baby around, the ladies would flock in here. How much do you want off?"

"Just a trim. So what should I do?"

"Make a decision."

"Thanks, that was helpful. Could you hand me my cup?"

Carole handed Edie her cup and, while Edie sipped, finished the cut. "Whatever you do, it'll work out."

"Maybe, but for the first time in my life, I don't know what to do. It's like I'm groping in the dark."

"Just like the rest of us. In this life, we help each other along. It isn't only children who need a village."

"How un–American."

"You need to read more history."

"I don't like this indecision," said Edie glancing at her watch, "I gotta get back, it's about time to feed Hillary. Thanks."

Edie gulped the rest of her hot chocolate then left through Carole's back door and started her jog home. She sprinted past the Halloween house. When she reached the empty store, she walked, entranced by the millions of stars that could be seen when away from city lights.

At her front door, she took in a deep breath—she could smell winter in the wind. Thoughts of snuggling near the wood stove with Phil and Hillary made her warm, but images of Russell Washington's body popped into her brain and pushed everything else out. There was work to be done, she said to herself and hoped that the case wouldn't get uglier, that this would be the only death. She opened her door, and there was Phil on the couch wrapped in a blanket, waiting for her—asleep.

4

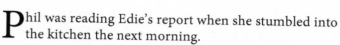

Phil was reading Edie's report when she stumbled into the kitchen the next morning.

"Have a seat; I'll get you a cup of coffee."

"Thanks, just juice," said Edie laying her head on the counter. "I'm off coffee this week, Hillary's reacting to something, and the parenting blogs suggest coffee as a possible culprit."

"What about dairy, wheat, nuts?"

"You read the blogs, too!"

"In my spare time. Better than calling my sisters or mother and asking them for advice. I'd be on the phone for hours, if I did that." Phil handed a glass of grape juice to her. "Your report is good."

"Had plenty of time last night to write and rewrite, Hillary was up two, no, three times last night. I'm beginning to understand why sleep deprivation is a major form of torture."

"Didn't hear a thing last night, slept like a baby."

"Not like our baby. Didn't you feel me punching you? Night is your time to get up."

"Wondered why my arm was sore this morning. And the deal was I'd take over nights when your maternity leave was done." Phil paused, "It isn't over, is it?"

"Sorry, no decision—yet."

"May I suggest that you continue with maternity leave and stay home? Sleep in. Get to know our baby better," said Phil, challenging history. The Edie he had come to know had one speed and one direction: fast and forward, she was an unstoppable force. And yet, *please stay with Hillary, please*, slipped from his brain into his mouth.

"Nice try. Those are all in my pro-column."

"You'll tell me when you've made a decision?"

"You'll be the second one to know."

"Who'll be the first?"

"Me."

Phil poured the pot of coffee into his thermos, and then scrounged through the fridge for leftovers for lunch. He kissed Edie good–bye, and then went to kiss Hillary. The doorbell rang, "I'll get it," he yelled from the bedroom, he picked up Hillary and went to answer the door.

"Hello, Mrs. Voss."

"Oh, what a beautiful baby," gushed Mrs. Voss. "May I hold her? Please, call me Sera."

Phil and Mrs. Voss did a juggling act as Phil handed her Hillary, then took the package and threw it on the couch. "Edie's in the kitchen. It's—"

"Don't bother, I know the way. Been in this house plenty of times," said Mrs. Voss, walking toward the kitchen and cooing at Hillary like an old pro.

Edie heard the exchange. She glanced around the room. The counter was covered with dishes from breakfast and last night's supper and, Edie saw, the lunch dishes from yesterday. How did the time get away from her? Edie quickly pulled open the dishwasher, hoping that activity might give Mrs. Voss the idea that she was on top of things.

"Good morning, Mrs. Voss. Sera, that's a pretty name, family name?"

"It is a family name, short for Seraphina. Lots of women with that name, on both sides of the family. Can't stand the name. But since my parents never consulted me, I make do. Please, call me Sera.

"But you like the name now?"

"Hell, no. Didn't you hear me tell Phil to call me Sera? By the way, you can call me that, too."

"Thanks. Want a cup of coffee? I think Phil left some."

"No thanks, had a cup at home. Saw you on TV last night."

"Dead man, don't know anything else."

"I'm that obvious?"

"Part of the job, it's what people always want to know. When they find out that I'm a cop, they think I know everything that is going on in the county and that I will give them the 'inside' information."

"What can I say? We're a small community, and the only entertainment we get is knowing each other's business . . . sometimes that isn't a bad thing."

"What about privacy?"

"Then you moved to the wrong neighborhood."

The phone rang. "Excuse me a moment," Edie said as she answered it. "Yeah, I can come in. Give me some time to not stink. I'll be there within the hour."

"You have a landline?"

"Keep it to screen my calls. My cell's only for friends and some family members," said Edie. She looked at Hillary sleeping in Mrs. Voss's arms. "Would you mind holding her while I take a shower?"

"Not at all. It'll give me my grandmother fix."

"Thanks." Edie sped to the bathroom. Moments later, Edie was back, dressed and brushing her hair.

"That didn't take long," said Mrs. Voss, handing Hillary to her.

"The day is just starting, I'll waste time later, after my work is done. Thanks."

"You're a good writer."

"You read my report?"

"It was right side up on the counter. I'm only human. Hillary was sleeping, and I needed something to do. Looks like an interesting case."

"I'm afraid of that."

"Why?"

"I found the body. My boss knows that I like to finish what I start and that this case has the potential to be very interesting. She's asked me to come back early from maternity leave. I don't know what to do."

"Tough decision. If you need any help with Hillary, call me, I'd be happy to help."

"Thanks," said Edie, buckling Hillary into her car seat.

When Edie walked into Gracie Davis's office, she still didn't know if she was going to accept the lieutenant's offer. This indecision was killing her guts, she'd have to make a decision soon or start popping Tums.

Gracie looked up, "It's good sense to knock before entering this office."

"Sorry, thought you wanted to meet."

"We do. You know most of these people, except Prescott Marr from Homeland Security. Everyone, you remember Edie Swift, she was the first on the scene."

Wow, thought Edie, this is really hot property. Russell Washington must've been more than just an FBI agent. "Only agency missing is the CIA," she said.

"That would be Russell Washington, but he's dead," said Gracie.

Edie hoped that she was in control of her legendary poker face. "Thought he was FBI?"

"He was doing some educational work with the CIA, some work on terrorism. They're satisfied that I will keep them informed," said Fred Price from the FBI.

"You guys actually talk to each other?" said Edie.

"At times," said Fred.

Hillary began to cry. Edie found a chair in the corner, behind everyone, raised her T-shirt and guided Hillary to the nipple. Everyone turned to watch Gracie throw her sweater over Edie's shoulder, hiding Hillary.

"What's that for?" said Edie.

"Decency, in my time we went to the ladies' room to nurse our babies," said Gracie.

"No one has to watch."

"When a woman shows a boob, everyone watches."

"If you want me on the case, this is what you got to work with."

"You on the case?" asked Gracie.

"Depends on what I hear today," said Edie. "But I'm not hearing anything at the moment."

"Okay, let's get this thing rolling," said Gracie. "Who's first?"

"We want to know what's been found," Fred Price said.

"Edie, looks like you're first up," said Gracie.

"It's all in the report, but since I only made one copy, I'll talk you through it. Phil Best," Edie didn't know how to explain him, *my lover and father of my child, boyfriend was for someone younger than her, significant other, would boy toy be too shocking for the men in the room;* she didn't know in which century these men had parked their brains or morals, better to play it safe, she had to work with them. She settled on the innocuous phrase. "My significant other, our daughter, and I went to Indian Lake Park to hike. There was one car in the parking lot when we came in. I saw no one in the front part of the park. Phil saw someone pulling a boat leave from the other end of the lake."

"Why did he see it and not you?" asked Agent Marr.

"I was sleeping," stated Edie.

"Why?" Marr pressed.

"Because I have a newborn, and I sleep every chance I get."

"Why?"

"Exactly how old are you? Did you hear a word I said? I surmise that either you have never had children or you let you wife handle the entire child care." Edie didn't let Marr reply. "If the former is the case, you did your children a favor."

"Enough of this schoolyard bickering," said Lieutenant Davis. "As I mentioned, Edie's on maternity leave. Continue with you report, Edie. Please."

Edie continued, but kept a watchful eye on Agent Marr. "We heard screams, and then saw two girls come running off the hill. While Phil called 9-1-1, I went to investigate. What I saw was a bloody mess of a man. Checked for a carotid pulse to make sure he was dead. He was," Edie added to head off any more of what she considered were Marr's stupid questions. "When Lieutenant Davis came on scene, she, two deputies, Ben Harris, and I followed his bloody trail to where we assume the crime was committed. Then we followed a trail that we assume was used to gain entrance to the park, it came out on a farmer's field. That is the end of the report."

"That's it?" said Richard Norby, assistant US deputy attorney. "I was hoping for more details."

"Ask the scene investigators and medical examiner. I reported what I saw and heard," said Edie.

"Which wasn't much," said Prescott Marr. "Thank you for your input, but I think it more important we proceed with the detective on this case."

"Who's Phil?" asked Einer Niskanen, the attorney from the Wisconsin attorney general's office.

"My significant other," said Edie, certain now that seeing her nurse Hillary had caused the men's brains to freeze.

It was confirmed during the next hour as they peppered her with questions. Seeing a woman nursing must have turned off one brain and started another. They hadn't heard anything she said. Read the report, Edie wanted to yell, but saw Gracie direct a you–better–not stare in her direction.

"Well, Edie, what do you think? You going to take on this case?" asked Gracie when the questions trickled to a few.

"Who would I be working with?"

"Me," said Fred.

"Excuse me a moment, I need to step out in the hall for a second," said Edie placing Hillary in Gracie's arms.

"Now you want some privacy," said Gracie.

Edie left Gracie's office and went to search for a deserted room. She couldn't find one. She had to use the women's room. She checked that each stall was empty before punching Phil's number. He had wanted to be the first to know her decision.

"Pick up, pick up," she said to the phone. She got his phone message instead. "Phil, this is your notice, I'm taking this case. Hope you get it before I say yes to Gracie. If not, I love you."

Edie walked back into Gracie's office. "Yes, I'm on the job with all the conditions I asked for yesterday."

"I'll call personnel, see what I can do," said Gracie. "While I'm doing that, talk with these fellows."

"Now, I need some information. Tell me about Russell Washington," asked Edie.

"He was an expert on terrorism," said Marr.

"Washington's married, his wife is out of the country, we have our embassy in Kenya looking for her," said Fred.

"We want to be kept in the loop," said Norby. "We want to know if this was racially motivated, a possible civil rights case."

Edie bit her tongue. Of course it was a civil rights case. Someone took away his life, she thought.

"Wisconsin attorney general wants to know what is going on in his state," said Niskanen. "We expect to be kept informed . . . in a timely manner."

"Edie and Fred will keep you informed," said Gracie. "If there is nothing else, I've got work to do. Edie, stay here for a moment, I'd like a word with you."

"Yes. Fred, can you wait in the break room? I'd like to do some planning," said Edie.

"I'll wait," said Fred, before following the others out of the office.

Gracie settled Hillary into one arm, walked to the door to make certain that no one standing near it, and then closed the door. Then she cooed to Hillary. "Edie, are you certain you want to take this case?"

"All that for one little question?"

"Those men can smell uncertainty; they'll walk all over you, if they can. That man was found dead in my county. I want my people to lead the team, not mop up after those guys. Are you up to it?"

"I said I'd take the case."

"Just making sure," said Gracie. "Talking from experience, motherhood changes your perspective and wreaks havoc with your sleep. You need to be at the top of your game. Can you do it?"

"Yes. I've got people lined up to help with Hillary and where there are voids, Phil will have to do more than his share for a while."

"Good. If you need any help, give me a call."

Edie stood to leave. "That baby's mine," she said.

"And I'll keep her until after you're done at the autopsy," Gracie said.

"Damn. I forgot about that."

"Watch your mouth."

"And you just remember to give that baby back when I'm done at the medical examiner's."

Gracie leaned over Hillary and took in a deep breath of the new baby scent. "Maybe."

"Didn't know babies were so addictive," said Edie.

"They are. I have a few to prove it," said Gracie.

"Maybe I should talk to your daughters about supplying you with grandbabies."

"No, you don't. They need to finish college, get jobs, move out of my house, and find husbands before they have children."

"It doesn't always work that way," said Edie.

"If my family knows what's good for them, they'd better be walking the straight and narrow as defined by me," said Gracie, as she caressed Hillary's downy hair. "Now get out of here. We've got work to do. I'll call the medical examiner to tell them you are coming."

Fred was waiting for Edie just outside Lieutenant Davis's office. He stood up when he saw Edie emerge. "Got a scolding from the principal?" asked Fred.

"From that old softie? She just wanted Hillary to herself. Now she gets her for about an hour."

"Didn't know she had a soft spot."

"She does, but never mention it to her."

"Noted," said Fred.

"Want to take in the autopsy?"

"Was headed that way, wasn't sure that you would be going."

"Why? I didn't become squeamish when I became a mother."

"I didn't think that. The mothers I know are tougher than the fathers. Glad you decided to take the case. How's the family doing?"

"Good, except Phil doesn't like that I'm interested in this case."

"He knew what he was getting himself into before you two took up housekeeping."

"That he did," Edie said, laughing. "With this case, I'm not sure I do. I thought they were going to waterboard me back there."

"I wouldn't have let them."

"Thanks," said Edie, pushing the down elevator button.

"Don't worry about those guys; get men together and they try to see who has the biggest dick . . . without actually putting it on display," said Fred.

"They should've taken a piss together; there'd be no question about size then."

"They haven't crossed streams since they were little boys. Seriously, Edie," said Fred, holding the elevator door for Edie. "You can see that this is a big case. We don't know anything. That is scary. We don't know if this was done by some racially motivated punks, or if it was gang-related or related to Russell Washington's job. We don't know."

"I get that. I hate not knowing. I hate waiting. But that is what I have to do. What else can I do? Demanding results isn't going to solve this case. It will only be solved by us pounding the beat, see what shakes loose, and then go from there. What are you going to do?"

"Wait and hope that Russell Washington's wife can fill in some detail so we can get the ball rolling on this case."

"Not much planning to do now, is there? Call when you've talked to Mrs. Washington."

"And you'll call me, if anything develops?" quizzed Fred, uncertain of Edie's response. He knew from experience she liked to work alone.

"Of course, we're a team," said Edie, taking the diaper bag from Fred. "Thanks."

Gracie called the autopsy room to remind Edie that she and Hillary were waiting. It was tough for Edie to pull herself away. Before, she had always stayed to the end of the autopsy. As the primary detective on the case, it took about an hour to complete the chain of evidence duties. Today, it was different, she had another job to do—parenting.

Edie stepped out into the autumn sunshine, Hillary secure in the sling, diaper bag hanging from one shoulder and the car seat dangling from a hand. "Welcome to Madison, Sweetie, your birthplace, my hometown. We'll ditch the car seat, and I'll show you around."

They walked past the Monona Terrace. "That building spoils the view," Edie whispered to her daughter. "When I was a little girl, I could look straight at Lake

Monona. What view do I get now? Another damned building. If you think I'm bad, mention this building to your Aunt Jill and you'll see Fourth of July fireworks." Edie looked around at the explosion of high rises. She knew that a city either grew up or out. She didn't like urban sprawl. But she also didn't like her Madison growing beyond a human scale. "Second thought, let's go home."

Edie secured the car seat, and then buckled Hillary into it. Somewhere in the ramp was a car that needed a muffler, she lifted her head trying to see the car as it exited the ramp. She couldn't. "Someone needs to tell that guy to fix his muffler." Edie finished buckling Hillary's car seat and left the ramp.

5

*

Edie almost drove past the mall. "Where the hell is my brain?" she said softly to herself and quickly maneuvered into the right turn lane as car horns blasted around her. She needed new clothes, the pre–pregnancy ones didn't fit and she no longer wanted to be seen in her pregnant clothes. And she needed something else, but she couldn't remember what it was; Edie was sure she'd remember once she saw the item. "Sorry, little one, but we're making a quick stop here, Mama needs a few things."

Edie pulled the stroller from the trunk, unlatched Hillary's car seat, and then secured it in the stroller. Edie shook her head; maybe if she had played with dolls as a kid, she'd know how to work all these baby gadgets.

The buggy brigade was in full force at the mall. Kids running everywhere as their exasperated mothers tried to keep pace with and corral them, and Edie trying to figure out which store carried mommy stuff. She dodged a toddler pushing a stroller which was aimed at Hillary and stepped into the nearest store. At least, she thought, she was safe from power hungry toddlers. And, after looking around, she thought this store might have what she needed.

Edie was deep into comparing nursing bras when someone moved close to her—no one had been there before, she had thought her part of the store had been empty. Edie turned to see two young women quickly move to another clothes rack near her. Edie checked her purse, still there and not open. She stared at the girls long enough to be able to describe them, if needed, and then noticed that both girls were staring in one direction. Edie turned to follow their gaze. Nothing. Only clothes racks. But Edie was certain that someone had been there, that those girls had been taking cues from someone. She reached into her cavernous diaper bag in search of her cell. She wasn't finding it. She was certain that she had thrown it in there at the office. Edie looked down, the cell was resting inside a diaper. She pulled it out. Dead. When Edie turned back toward the girls, they were gone. Edie decided it was time to leave. That choice was confirmed when she heard police sirens wailing to a stop outside the store.

She grabbed a bra and proceeded to the checkout. Edie looked for the girls while waiting in line. Nowhere, they were nowhere to be seen. But seeing two Madison police officers walking through the doors, she guessed that the girls had been caught with their hands in someone's purse.

"That is sad," said the clerk.

"What is?" asked Edie.

"Cops in the store. Someone was probably caught shoplifting. That problem gets worse as we get closer to the holidays. They're starting early this year; second time this week we've had cops in the store."

"Hope that's all they were doing?"

"The cops?"

"No, the . . . whoever was shoplifting. You know, sometimes it's a gateway crime. Start out with small crimes and increase to more serious stuff until that's how they make their living. And somewhere in there, somehow the criminal starts to blame the victim for the crime, weird."

"Really? How do you know?"

"I listen to public radio," said Edie, handing over her credit card. There was no reason to tell the clerk that she was a cop; that she'd seen many petty criminals make the step to major crimes. Plus, whenever she mentioned that she was a cop, people seemed to silently review their sins, hoping that none showed, and then, as soon as they could, got busy with something else— usually far, far away from her. At times, it made her feel like a priest: in front of her, people were on their best behavior, when her back was turned, they lapsed into being human. She stopped mentioning that she was a cop a long time ago.

"Wish I could listen to that, but they only play music here. Stuff to keep the customers happy. Soon it will be Christmas music, looped continuously."

"Sounds wonderful," said Edie, taking back her card and placing the bag at Hillary's feet.

"It is, but only for the first fifteen times."

Edie wanted to get Hillary out of the mall, but she was more curious about the girls. She pushed the stroller toward the store's office. The doors were closed. She couldn't think of any reason to enter. Time to go, she'd ask about this incident next time she was downtown.

6

*

Phil sat at the counter staring at Edie as she prepared his favorite, beef stroganoff.

"What are you staring at?" Edie asked.

"You."

"Why?

"I'm waiting to hear what you decided. But since you're making one of my favorite meals, I already know."

Edie turned from the stove, exasperated, "Didn't you listen to my message? Why do I bother leaving any messages? And you complain about me not using my cell phone!"

Phil searched his pockets for his phone. "Must have left my phone in the truck." He got up from the counter.

"Sit down; you can get your phone after we eat. I'll deliver the message in person. I'm taking the job. You can confirm later that you were the second person to know."

Phil sat quietly. "My mother said you would."

"You discussed this with your mother!"

"As if you don't consult Aunt Jill about everything."

"Not about this," said Edie, dumping the egg noodles into the boiling water. She was rewarded with a splash-back of scalding water. "What else did your mother say?"

Phil pulled an ice pack from the freezer and applied it to Edie's forearm. "She'd be happy to watch Hillary. And why isn't she baptized yet? And the bigger question, when are we getting married? No, I think that comes before Hillary not being baptized." Phil thought for a moment. "No, that's the right order. Mom's old school; after the baby's born, to hell with the mother. I've got the milk, why buy the cow."

"I'm not chattel. Anything else?"

"No, she wanted to know about the dead man."

"And—"

"I'm not stupid. And I remembered your warning. I didn't tell her anything." Phil put his arms around her, and nibbled on her ear. "Are you sure you don't want to stay with Hillary?"

Edie felt herself melt. "Of course, I want to stay with Hillary. But I also want to catch whoever killed that man."

"Why you? Why does it always have to be you?"

"It isn't always me. Why not me? When the bonds holding us together as a community are torn, I do society's dirty work of finding the culprit. I help clean up the mess. What I do gives a modicum of justice to the injured, a sense of order back to a community. This job is important to me."

"Isn't Hillary?"

"Yes. Why do I have to choose? Why don't you quit your job to stay home with her?"

Edie had backed Phil into a corner. No, he'd put himself there. The only way out was the truth or what part of it that he cared to reveal. "I just want to keep my family safe."

"We've been over this ground before. I'm not the little woman. I'm a cop and have been one for a while now. I know how to take care of myself. And you are not the only one concerned about this family's safety. That is part of why I choose to do this job."

"So, you are your brother's keeper."

"That is not a sin. We all are, some take it too far, but we all safeguard each other. Read your Bible."

"Didn't know you went to church."

"No one believes that. Most think I'm a pagan or worse."

"The worst, for Mom, is being raised by hippies."

"I was raised by hippies and wasn't baptized. A double whammy. I knew there were sound reasons for why she hates me."

"I thought it was because you had corrupted her little boy."

"Her little boy didn't need my help."

"So, I can give my mother an answer next time she asks, why we aren't married yet."

"If she doesn't like me, why push us to get married?"

"She thinks it would benefit Hillary, a moral upbringing. And you are evading the question."

"Tell your mother we're waiting until Hillary can be our flower girl."

"That sounds as if we've set a date."

"Take it as you want to. Dinner is ready.

7

✳

Hillary was asleep in her swing; Edie was at the
kitchen table making to-do lists when Mrs. Voss
knocked, and then walked into the kitchen.

"Sorry to barge in, still used to when Gladys Heyden
owned it. I'll try to remember from now on not to do
that. I brought some cookies as a peace offering," she
said setting the plate near Edie.

"Do you Troutbeck people always barge into
homes?" asked Edie.

"Some of us do. Most of us in this little community
grew up around here, went to church here. We're probably all shoestring relatives. And walking into homes un-
announced is the best way to look for skeletons in each
other's closets."

"I'll keep that in mind. Thanks for the cookies. But
next time yell when you open the door so I know you're
in the house. You might see my gun, before you see me."

"I'll try to call out first," said Mrs. Voss. "Mind if I
admire your baby?"

"Admire away. Just don't wake her."

Mrs. Voss pulled a chair over near Hillary's swing.
Edie went back to her lists.

"She sleeping through the night yet?" asked Mrs. Voss.

"She did last night. First good sleep I've had since her birth."

"Did you hear that car last night?"

"What time was that?"

"After I went to sleep and before I got up this morning."

"Nope."

"Really, I bet you can hear Hillary when she wakes up."

"Yes, but I was exhausted last night."

"Wouldn't worry, it'll get better until your kid gets a car—then you never see her until she graduates from high school."

"It can't be as bad as that."

"Just giving you a heads-up. Enjoy her now when you know where she is. What are you working on?"

"Lists of sitters and everyday stuff I'll need to pack for Hillary. I'm on this case."

"What does Phil think?"

"Hates it. Probably hates it more when he has to babysit."

"Could I be on the list of sitters?"

"Maybe, if you can clear a criminal background check. If you pass that, you'd come after Aunt Jill, Carole Rhyme, my boss, a couple of Phil's sisters, Phil's mom."

"All that for a baby?"

"Yes."

"But there's always a chance—"

"Yes, but if something happens, I want to know that it is chance and not my screwup."

Mrs. Voss thought it better to change the subject, "Phil's mom comes last! What's her name?"

"Lorraine Best. To be blunt, we don't see eye to eye. But since Hillary is Phil's daughter, she might be reliable."

"Hmmm."

"What's that for? Do you know her?"

"Possibly, there's a few by that name in the area."

"She does come from a big family. So did her husband," said Edie looking up from her lists as Hillary let out a soft whimper.

"Mind if I hold her?"

"It would be a big help. I might be able to finish these lists."

Mrs. Voss unbuckled Hillary, and took her to the living room to rock her. Edie worked on her lists while enjoying a few of Mrs. Voss's cookies. A phone ringing somewhere in the house interrupted her. Edie found it on the last ring. Checking the caller ID, Edie saw it was from Gracie Davis. She had to answer it.

"Hi, Gracie. I gotta keep working here, so I have you on speaker phone," Edie said.

"Learning to multitask?" Gracie asked.

"I know how to do that. I'm learning how to incorporate a new life into the one I already have. Who knew that someone so little could be so demanding? What can I do for you?" Edie asked, as she returned to her lists.

"Need you to interview one of the cleaning ladies at The Morning Rose."

"Now?"

"Yes. I'm feeling some heat on this case. It has to be today."

"I need to find a sitter for Hillary. Can you take her?"

"No."

"Can I take Hillary to the interview?"

"Not the wisest move. But . . . this should just be a routine interview."

"Don't know if I have a choice. Phil's on the road. Aunt Jill hasn't changed shifts," Edie thought for a moment. "Let me get this straight. This is a routine interview and I can take Hillary, if I must."

"You didn't hear that from me."

"I know . . . I know."

"Thanks," said Gracie.

Edie flipped the phone shut. What to do with Hillary?

Mrs. Voss spoke up. "Can I help?"

Edie assessed Mrs. Voss. What did she know about her? She is a neighbor. She's about the age of Aunt Jill and Lorraine Best. She doesn't like the name Seraphina. Nothing. Edie knew nothing about this friendly looking neighbor.

"Maybe. I've got to interview someone and I'm trying to figure out what to do with Hillary."

"I could stay here with her."

"Thanks for the offer, but I think I'll take her with me today," Edie quickly added. Could you change her while I'm getting ready? That would make my day go faster."

"Yes. Which room is hers?"

"She still sleeps in our room, but everything you'll need is in the nursery." Mrs. Voss looked confused. "Down the hallway, door's open to her room. You should find everything you need there."

"I think I can find my way," said Mrs. Voss, taking Hillary to the room.

"Thanks," said Edie as she checked the diaper bag for all the essentials. Gun was in its holster, safety on. Diapers, check. Dirty diaper bag, check. Extra clothes for Hillary and herself, check. Cell phone, check. Soft baby carrier, check. She placed the breast pump on the counter, won't need that today. Then chose her outfit: black maternity slacks, a white T–shirt and a bulky wrap–style cardigan.

By the time Edie was out of the shower and dressed, Mrs. Voss had Hillary changed and strapped into the car seat.

"You work fast."

"Experience. Need anything else? I'd be happy to help."

"I think I've got it," said Edie, shouldering the diaper bag and lifting the car seat. "Could you get the door for me?"

"Certainly," said Mrs. Voss.

8

✳

Edie drove around the block on which The Morning Rose was located a few times before a parking spot opened. Why were there so many cars near campus when everyone walked to class? She skillfully slid into the spot, got Hillary into the front carrier and hoisted the diaper bag onto her shoulder.

The hotel was charming, one of the few mansions in downtown Madison that had escaped being chopped into student apartments. The front porch was broad, Edie thought it might be possible to sit there during a downpour and not get wet, charming. The interior was homey, it invited people to grab a paper and flop down on one of the chairs or couches. Edie placed the diaper bag in a corner as her claim to that space. With her back to the wall, she could monitor the comings and goings of the inn from there. Then she went in search of the manager. He was a little disconcerted to see a cop wearing a baby; nothing like that would ever touch his clothing, but he quickly recovered and went in search of the maid who had been on duty over the weekend.

When he returned with the maid, Edie was nursing Hillary.

"We have another room where you might be more comfortable feeding your baby," Nathan Blair said, blushing.

"You apologize to this woman right now," demanded the maid. "Or I will be filing a complaint with the city attorney concerning this discrimination. This is Madison; the law clearly states she has every right to nurse her baby wherever she chooses. I can have fifty people here tonight demonstrating against this injustice."

"I'm sorry, ma'am. I didn't quite understand the law. Are you comfortable? May I bring you something to drink?" Blair asked.

"Water would be fine, thank you," Edie replied. As he left Edie heard him mumbling about having to hire students who always knew their rights and were willing to back them up.

"I'm Kirsten Sather; I was one of the maids on duty last weekend. What can I do for you?" Kirsten said as she took a chair across from Edie.

"I'm Edie Swift, detective with the Dane County Sheriff Department. You stood your ground with your boss."

"I'm a maid, not a slave. If you don't stand up for your rights, you never know when that right will disappear."

"I'm guessing you are a student. Do you have to worry about losing this job?"

"Yes, I'm a student—a junior. No, I don't have to worry about losing this job. I think the inn has to worry about retaining me."

"Why is that?"

"There aren't many people who want to do this job."

"They could hire illegals."

"True. But they probably won't. That practice would be tolerated by some in this part of town, but here, it's too conspicuous. This company wouldn't try it—they want to build a reputation of being an upstanding community company."

"Just curious, have you declared a major yet?"

"No. I will have to choose one, soon."

"With your insight and willingness to stand up to and for people, ever thought about a course of study that would fit with law enforcement? We could use a few more like you."

"I'll keep that in mind."

"Good. Let's get started." Edie put a picture of Russell Washington on the table. "Can you identify this man?"

"That is Russell Washington," Kirsten said.

"How do you know him?"

"He was pointed out to me by the manager on duty that day, Nathan Blair."

"Why did he point him out?"

"I was told to take special care of him and his room."

"Meaning what?"

"A thorough cleaning of his room and when he was at the hotel, wait on him hand and foot."

"Was he with anyone?"

"No one that I saw."

"I'm interested in anything you heard, saw or knew about Russell Washington. Can you expand on the hours you worked last weekend?"

"I came in to work at approximately ten in the morning, left at approximately three."

"Did you clean Russell Washington's room?"

"Yes. It didn't need much cleaning; it was more like I straightened it up. He was a very tidy man. I made the bed, put out fresh towels, set out another bottle of water, checked the bathroom, vacuumed, and then left the room."

"What do you mean he was tidy?"

"His toiletries were set out in an orderly fashion in the bathroom. The towels were folded. He placed his newspaper, which was neatly folded, in the recycle basket. His shoes were lined up."

"Could you tell if more than one person had slept in the bed?"

"I assumed one."

"Why is that?"

"Only one side of the bed needed to be straightened. The other side was undisturbed."

"You notice a lot. What about Sunday?"

"Nothing to clean or straighten. He hadn't been in his room since the day before. More precisely, that is what I assumed to have happened."

"How could you tell?"

"In my rooms, I do origami with the towels and set them on the bed. The origami I did on Saturday was still on the bed when I entered Sunday morning. It hadn't been moved."

"He could have set it off the bed then returned it to the bed. Anything else that would suggest he hadn't been in his room?"

"Yes. He hadn't used the bathroom. The end tissue of the toilet paper was still folded in those neat little triangles that we have to fold when we're done cleaning the bathroom. The towels were still folded. And the cookie wasn't eaten."

"What cookie?"

"This hotel caters to wealthy alumni, so when there's a home game the chef makes guerilla cookies—a holdover from the sixties."

"It wasn't that long ago, I remember those cookies from when I was a little girl."

"Anyway, we put a cookie for each guest in the rooms, his was still uneaten—I've never seen that happen before."

"Did you ever meet Russell Washington?"

"No. As I said, he was pointed out to me by Nathan Blair."

"Do you know if anyone came back to his room with him?"

"Don't know, but I doubt it. When I made his bed on Saturday, it looked as if only one person had used it. The blankets were tossed back on one side, the other side unused. Nothing wild was going on in that room Friday night."

"Do you have anything else to add?"

"No."

"You have answered my questions succinctly."

"My daddy taught us to answer briefly and only to answer the question asked us of us, so as not to get sidetracked."

"What kind of work is your father in?"

"He's a defense attorney."

"Are you following in his footsteps?"

"Don't know, yet. But he has me marked for a Supreme Court justice."

"If you change your mind, you'd fit in well with law enforcement."

"Talk to my daddy."

Kirsten went back to her work. Edie went in search of the manager. She wanted to get into the room, to see for herself what Kirsten had just told her.

"Someone from your department is already there, but let me show you to the room."

Edie followed, admiring the period antiques as they climbed the stairs.

"Is The Morning Rose ADA compliant?" asked Edie.

"The owners lucked out with that. The house was originally built with an elevator. We just had to make a few minor adjustments."

"They did a wonderful restoration job."

"Yes, they did. It was bought because one of the owners was tired of seeing these wonderful old Mansion Hill homes chopped into student housing. Students could never appreciate something this wonderful," Blair said as he admired the crystals hanging from the sconces. Frowning, he took out his breast pocket handkerchief and wiped a fingerprint from one of the crystals, and then expertly folded it and returned it to his pocket. "Here we are. This was Mr. Washington's room." He left Edie standing at the closed door.

Edie knocked before she entered the room. Sadie Carpenter, with camera in hand, walked out of the bathroom.

"Oh, it's you," said Sadie. "And you brought your baby to a crime scene. Again. Stay where you are. I haven't released this scene."

"This is not the crime scene," said Edie, but stood in the doorway as instructed.

"It could be."

"We found the body out at Indian Lake. Didn't expect to find another one here. Tell me, what's the holdup at Indian Lake?"

"Thoroughness. And I think I'm done here. You may have the room and key."

"What about Indian Lake?"

"We'll let Lieutenant Davis know when we are done," said Sadie as she packed up her equipment.

Edie waited for Sadie to leave before doing her own search of the room. She wished there were incantations she could invoke to ward off the evil spirits Sadie Carpenter seemed to lug with her and leave behind.

The room was, as Kirsten had said, tidy. Nothing was out of place. Edie opened drawers; there were a few neatly folded shirts, jeans, some socks, and some tidy whities. No clothes in the closet. It looked as if he came for just a few days. Clothes, neatly folded, were all that remained of Russell Washington. From such meager belongings, Edie could not extrapolate anything new. He was a tidy man, if not fastidious.

As Edie left the inn, Nathan Blair handed her a bottle of water, with a smile.

9

*

The deal was that Edie would only work the Russell Washington case then go back on her maternity leave. It was either a convoluted idea or an underhanded trick, thought Phil. Edie could not keep her fingers out of other cases; once on the job, she would stay.

Three days after the crime Edie was still cursing the crime scene people for not finishing their on-site work. Didn't they know that this was fall in Wisconsin? Indian summer wasn't going to last forever. Rain would set in soon with snow and ice following.

She called Fred twice that day. First to tell him about the interview with Kirsten Sather, that there was nothing to discover at the hotel except that Russell Washington had been a tidy person. She'd learned nothing from the inn's personnel. The second time was to learn more about his quests: No, Mrs. Washington had not contacted him or the embassy. Yes, he'd call her when that happened.

The medical examiner, unfortunately for him, took Edie's call. He could only say what the stomach contents might be; the toxicology report would take longer. Cause of death, massive hemorrhaging. He'd call her when the tests were back, swearing not to take Edie Swift's phone calls until absolutely necessary.

The wait was driving Edie nuts. Maybe someone in the office needed her help. Then she remembered the discussions she had with Phil. Maybe this was the day she was to learn how to wait—maybe.

She couldn't. She had learned at a young age to take action, with her mother flitting around somewhere in the world, and Aunt Jill, her rock, needing to make a living for herself and Edie, it was solve your own problems or suck it up. There had been a time when she sucked it up and sat in a corner, hoping the problems would go away. Then came the day she decided to step out of the shadows. That she was 'it'. That she needed to solve her problems, because they weren't going away on their own. That it was just her and Aunt Jill against the world.

Then Phil came into her life. At first, it was just delicious weekends together that melted into sweet weeks together. And now, now they were three and Aunt Jill. She had let two more people, Phil and Hillary, into her space. When had that happened? And what was she going to do about it?

Nonsense! Waiting, she had always thought, was for the doctor's office or the DMV—not her. She packed up Hillary and headed to the office.

The few people in the office gathered around Edie, saying they were glad she was back, picking up Hillary, and playing pass–the–baby. As each person cradled her, they cooed at her, took a deep breath of that new baby smell, and passed her to the next person. Edie had never seen these seasoned cops melt so fast. Edie took advantage of her cop pals playing pass–the–baby and went to the crime scene people. No, they weren't done at the scene—check back, maybe tomorrow. Nothing unusual had come in over the past few days: drunks, drugs, car wrecks, domestic violence, rapes, a couple of midnight fights, Iowa County reported stolen firearms—nothing out of the ordinary. Edie hated the waiting game. If she was totally back, she thought, maybe she'd get involved in some of those "easy" cases. A few of them sounded interesting. But she wasn't back, she reminded herself. Only the Russell Washington case was on her plate, she continued to remind herself. Only the Russell Washington case, she sighed, and went back to Hillary.

The cops in the office were glad to see Edie leave; Edie with nothing to do was worse than Edie on the hunt.

Edie put Hillary in the front carrier and walked around the square; she hadn't had time to stroll the Capitol since she was a student. "That," she said to Hillary, "is our Capitol—the people's house. And that is what got me into this job—I wanted to do my part in keeping it the people's house and not home to some dictator, oligarch, or anyone else who'd take power away from the people. I wish some of the legislators would remember that. When you are older remember to ask Aunt Jill about her time on campus. She'll tell you all about the protests and riots then launch into the people who came to school and refused to leave. But you'll like her. You'll like this place, it isn't Moscow on Mendota, nor is it seventy-seven square miles surrounded by reality—that area is a lot more compact than that." Edie finished their walk around the square and her running commentary on what Madison used to be and the big city it was becoming. "Can't say I like that trend," she said as she buckled Hillary in for the ride home.

Day four after the crime, Edie cleaned her gun. She hadn't been to the firing range since well before Hillary was born. Maybe she should do that while she waited for the crime scene people to finish their work. Or maybe they needed her help. She already knew that Sadie Carpenter needed all the help she could get; maybe the others did, too.

Night didn't bring any relief. Edie sat in the kitchen watching the darkness grow.

"What has gotten into you?" Phil asked. "You can't sit still. You can't finish a project. Although the house does look cleaner than when we bought it."

"It's this Washington case. The crime lab people are taking a long time."

"It's a huge area."

"Then the department should have put more people on it."

"Did crime stand still for this case? Do they have the resources to keep everyone on this case? Is nothing else important? Give them a break. They all want to nail this case."

"Then let me do my job."

"They will. When they're done with theirs."

"I hate waiting. I want to see the site again. I try to put myself back there on that day, see if it will give me some clues as to why this murder. And I want to get this case done and get back to my leave." Edie knew that was only half the truth. It bugged her that she stipulated she would only work on the Washington case. What was worse was that Gracie Davis and the department were holding up their end of the bargain, this was the only case Edie was to work on. She wanted to be in on every case, if only as a sounding board, like it was before she went on leave. Right now, no one was coming to ask her advice—damn it. "I didn't realize how motherhood would affect me. I want to be back at work, and I want to be with Hillary."

"I'll solve your problem; tell Gracie you are off the case and maybe off the force."

"What?"

"You just said you can't decide between being a cop and parenting. I solved your dilemma. Your case is closed."

"But I like both. What about the mortgage, car payments, insurance, clothing, Hillary's education?"

"Then figure out how to do both. As for money, my trucking company is solid. We'll look for good health insurance, and we've already put a plan in place for Hillary's education. I'm tired, I'm going to bed. You should, too."

"I'm not tired."

"Don't complain to me about being tired when Hillary reverts back to two feedings a night." Phil kissed Edie goodnight. There were some things that Edie Swift had to wrestle with herself.

Edie sat next to the wood stove and rocked and thought until the fire died down. When the flames became embers, she closed the flue, checked on Hillary, and then slipped into bed, curling around Phil.

But sleep did not come. Edie turned this way and that. She threw the blankets off. She pulled them back on. Nothing worked, she couldn't sleep. She snuggled up to Phil, kissed his neck, ran her hand under his T-shirt. She would never understand how men could only wear T-shirts to bed, especially on these cold nights. Her hand lingered over his six-pack abs.

Phil turned over to face Edie, "I fell asleep waiting for you."

"We're not sleeping now."

"You're sure this is okay?"

"All systems checked out fine," said Edie as Phil explored her body.

"That bra doesn't do a thing for me."

"I leak."

"Not a romantic image. At least I won't get sprayed."

"Welcome to the new reality."

"This isn't going to be one of those long nights . . . is it?"

"No, I think those times are gone. Just a quickie tonight. Never know when the baby will wake."

"I'm missing those times already. But I'll do what I can to oblige you."

It started slow but was over fast. Edie snuggled against Phil's chest and listened as his breathing slowed to a sleeping rate. Another thing I will never understand about men, she thought. How can they fall asleep so fast after sex? She never could. Edie rolled onto her back and thought about the Washington case. About her work. About Hillary. And about how she wasn't getting any sleep.

Edie did hear Hillary's cries, but she couldn't open her eyes or force herself out of bed. She lay in bed and listened for a moment trying to figure out what Hillary's cries meant: was the she hungry? Wet? Or did she just want to know she wasn't alone in the world? The cries got louder, and then Edie felt Phil place Hillary in her arms, put a pillow behind the baby, and covered them both with kisses and the blankets. It was a good night, he said, and then left for work. The baby slept. And so did Edie.

The phone finally ended Edie's sleep.

It was Gracie. "The crime lab is done. It's all yours. Call Fred."

Then the phone went dead. Edie collapsed back into bed and reordered her day.

10

❋

First, Edie changed Hillary, and then she called Aunt Jill to make sure she was available to care for Hillary. Then she packed the diaper bag, then stuffed her gun in the breast pump bag, then rechecked that there were enough bottles and cold packs for the expressed milk, and then ate. Her life had changed. Instead of stuffing her gun in its holster and chewing on a sandwich as she drove to a crime scene, she'd become a packhorse.

Edie looked in the backseat, hoping she hadn't forgotten Hillary. There she was, snug and comfortable in her car seat. It was then she remembered she needed to call Fred. She could do that while driving. She backed out of her drive, stopped for a combine, and then followed it, slowly, and called Fred. They arranged to meet at her office.

Edie talked to Hillary all the way into Madison, "Sweetie, I'm going back to work. You will be staying with Aunt Jill, you'll like her. Remember when she came to the hospital? It was very sweet of her. She'll take good care of you. Just like she took good care of me when I was a kid. You'll have lots of fun. I won't be at work very long. So you be a good girl while I'm away." Edie kept up the running commentary all the way into Aunt Jill's, and she hoped that some of what she was saying was true.

Aunt Jill was out of the house before Edie eased the car into the driveway, and she had the car seat out before Edie could open her door. All that was left for Edie to do was act as a pack mule, carrying all of the baby stuff she thought might be needed for Hillary's day, and follow Aunt Jill and Hillary into the house. Edie explained Hillary's day to Aunt Jill, and then handed her a detailed list of what she had just explained. Edie put the breast milk in the fridge, and handed Aunt Jill a manila envelope with every document that Eddie thought might be needed.

"She'll be fine," said Aunt Jill as she guided Edie to the door.

"Call if you need anything," said Edie, stepping outside. "My cell is on."

"I will," said Aunt Jill and closed the door. Edie felt a twinge of jealousy. She remembered the good years when Aunt Jill had taken care of her, when it was the two of them. For a moment, she wanted those years back. But she knew she couldn't have them. She was now an adult, she told herself. She was 'it.' And, not for the first time, Edie understood that there were things to do and miles to go before she could rest.

Edie sat behind the steering wheel and waved good-bye at Aunt Jill and Hillary as the two of them stood in the kitchen window, waving to her. She wiped away a tear, started the car, backed out of the driveway, and turned toward downtown Madison.

Edie's co-workers shouted hello, with a few calling out welcome back, when she walked into the department, and then they quickly retreated into their day's work.

They'd seen that Edie before, someone was in for a bad day. They were glad it wasn't them, but they were curious to see who was in Edie Swift's crosshairs. It didn't take long to find out the who—Sadie Carpenter walked into the room. It figured.

"Heard that this is going to be your case," said Sadie.

"So you decided to take your time."

"We combed the area, it's a big park. It's still closed off."

"And how many people obeyed that?"

"There's a patroller at the entrance to the park and other patrols are sent around the park on a regular basis."

"A challenge to every teen in the area: how can we screw with the cops and not get caught. A great story to be whispered in the bathrooms and locker rooms at school—how we outsmarted the Dane County cops."

"Not my problem. We did our part of the job. We collected everything that we thought might be part of this case," said Sadie, walking away. "The rest is up to you."

Edie and Fred were stopped by a sheriff's car at the entrance to the park.

"Excuse me, ma'am," the deputy said coming up to the car. "Oh, it's you. I can move my car, so you can drive in."

"Johnson . . . right?" Edie asked.

"Yes, ma'am."

"You been here long?"

"Just starting my shift. I like this assignment, quiet, nice scenery. Sure beats the dealings I've had with foul-mouthed teens earlier this week."

"Notice anyone stopping?"

"Not while I've been here. How long are you going to be?"

Edie looked at Fred, "Can't say, probably not past dusk."

"Take your time," said Johnson, then went to move his squad car.

The drive into the park was winding, grass was mowed, picnic shelter on the hill to the left looked untouched, the birch, hickory, and maple trees had dropped their leaves, and the oaks still clung to theirs. Not a spectacular view, but pleasant, thought Edie, as she parked her car. She reached back and lifted the bag with the breast pump forward. "Sorry, Fred, but I have to do this every two hours. You're welcome to sit here or, if you want, go check out the lake or something."

"I'll check out the lake. How long will it take?"

"If this thing works, about fifteen, twenty minutes."

"See you in twenty minutes." Fred walked away quickly so he wouldn't have to see Edie applying the pump to her breast. There were just some things that a cop didn't have to see. Blood, guts, severed limbs, bruised bodies, he had learned to look at without vomiting, but a woman with a breast pump he had no desire to see—ever.

Fred walked to the lake. It was a small lake with weeds around it; nice if you liked fishing. He didn't see any stones to skip. He walked back to the path that led up the hill and read the sign: Mary of the Oaks Chapel, erected by Peter Endres in thanks for sparing his family during a diphtheria epidemic, cared for by the Endres, Ballweg, and Marx families before becoming a Dane County Park. Fred looked around. At one time the chapel must have been visible from all approaches, but now the trees had repopulated the hill and obscured the chapel. What would Peter Endres think of trees covering his land, again? He turned and saw Edie get out of the car and stretch. He walked back down the hill toward the car. Edie met him halfway.

"Nice little park," said Fred.

"Yeah, it's pretty. Lived in Dane County all my life, but only made it out here last year. Since then, I vowed to come here once a year. I try to imagine what this place looked like before European settlers claimed the land. How often did the Indians pass this way? What did those settlers see in this land? Because all I see now are meandering roads, farm fields that are carved between hills and a lake. What were those people looking for? What were they fleeing? Why settle in this place?"

"Missed your calling, you should've been a history teacher."

"No, history is what I'm interested in, not what I want to do. Knowing the backstories, the stories of how people got to where they are when I step into their lives, does help me. But my calling is helping people deal with the now. What did Churchill say, the farther back you go—?"

"Churchill's always good for a quote," said Fred. "That's what you think we . . . cops do— help people deal with the here and now?"

"Yeah, but we deal with the seedier side of life, the side most of us want to deny, or at least forget. I think what I do is to bring a balance back to lives that are torn. Bring what justice I can to people who are grieving, scared. Give them a piece of stable ground to stand on as they readjust their lives."

"Makes us sound noble."

"Aren't we? We work on the razor's edge; we fall one way and everyone becomes evil—making a police state, a dictatorship more likely. We fall the other way, we're in danger of thinking everyone is a goodie–two–shoes and not being able to help bring back a sense of balance when the world tilts the wrong way."

"We're getting nobler by the minute. Doesn't everyone have a touch of evil in them?"

"Maybe, depends on the measuring tape. Enough of this grandiose talk, we're wasting daylight," said Edie as she started up the hill. Fred worked to keep up with her.

Edie slowed halfway up the hill. "This is where I met the girls and escorted them down. Second time I came up, I walked from this point. Saw nothing, no trampled undergrowth, nothing. But then it's hard to tell if anything was disturbed when the trees keep shedding their leaves."

"Ask them. They might stop for the noble Edie Swift."

"If only."

They stopped at the site where Russell Washington was found. Dust covered the blood-soaked ground. "The girls found him here. I checked for a carotid pulse, heard something snap, turned to find two guns pointed at me."

"Heard they were new guys."

"Scared. This was probably their first dead person."

"What happened next?"

"Four of us retraced his crawl to where we think the final act of violence took place," said Edie as she continued down the hill.

"Final?"

"Yeah, he may have died alone up here, but the beginning of his end started in another place. And there were many who were present at the end of his life. They split into two groups to come through the woods to this spot. There's a field road and standing corn at the end of these paths. Beyond that a township road. We think his end started in Madison, but we don't know how he got here and we don't know the whys and the who. Whoever did this was probably familiar with the area, but it's not safe to assume. So I'll start in Madison and work through the maze." Edie pondered the things that were yet to be discovered. "Have you heard from Washington's wife?"

"The embassy has located her; they just need to get her to a place with good Internet connections."

"Thought the whole world was connected."

"The Internet companies are trying, but for now some places are better connected than others. How many times do we lose a signal in *this* country?"

"Point taken. And this is the place where we think he was left to die," said Edie as she and Fred pushed their way into the clearing. She shook her head as if still not willing to believe what had happened there. If the blood were taken away, it looked like the campfires she had sat around when she was younger, minus the s'mores. Such profanity, she couldn't fathom; evil invading a place of beauty. "You know, I marvel at the human will. Without it he probably wouldn't have crawled out of here."

"He would have been well hidden."

"If he had stayed here we wouldn't have found him for months, maybe years—if ever. I am amazed that he got up that hill."

"Where do those paths ultimately get to, a paved road?"

"Yes, the township road."

"Anybody see anything?"

"Nothing, yet. Everyone in this area is busy getting the crops in, they can't take time to remember anything," said Edie as they followed the path to the field road. "Do you see anything?" she asked, looking around as they walked. "I don't see anything that could move us from Point A to Point B."

"Nada. Guess we have to wait for Mrs. Washington's interview and hope that she will give us something concrete. What's next for you?"

"Talking with people along these roads. Maybe they can stop long enough to focus on last week. Hopefully something will pop up," said Edie as she stared at what was left of the cornfield. She felt she was in the middle of a maze; she hadn't seen the beginning and couldn't see the end. *Damn, I hate mazes. Give me something.* "So what do we have on Mr. Washington?"

"Russell Washington, forty-eight years old, on loan to the CIA from the FBI, consulting on terrorism. Arrived from Atlanta, Georgia."

"Nothing new," Edie took a deep breath. "Better start beating the bushes."

"Can't see the forest for the trees, yet."

"Always darkest before the dawn."

"Except in about twenty minutes when the sun will set. Only light we'll have is my cell phone," said Edie.

"And mine," said Fred.

"They won't cut through the darkness; we'd better pick up the pace."

They made it back to the car as the sun set. Fred sat on the hood and watched the last light leave the sky while Edie pumped.

"It is quiet here," said Fred sliding into the passenger's seat. "If these residents didn't see anything, maybe they heard something?"

"Let's drive around this park, get a feel for the possibilities."

Edie drove around the park, didn't meet any cars. It was as if only she and Fred were in the world; she was glad to see the farmyard lights that pierced the dark, it made her feel a little less alone.

11

✻

Work, work, work...paperwork kept Edie's butt glued to her office chair. She read the reports from before and after Washington's death to prepare for the time when something, somebody, or maybe just a whisper moved this case forward.

Muggings, car thefts, joyrides, vandalism, store windows broken, rapes—the usual. She leaned back in her chair, sipped her coffee, and stared into the distance, hoping that her confusion would be mistaken for doggedness. Waiting was frustrating. Maybe she should have cut her leave short, just come back full time. She'd have other stuff to work on instead of this waiting game. Give her brain a rest from the case.

Smith brought her some relief when he stopped by her desk, "This might interest you, a cross burning. Might not be anything. This close to Halloween, weird stuff starts to happen."

"Sounds promising. Where and when?" asked Edie.

"Last night, somewhere along the Wisconsin River."

"That narrows it down to four-hundred-thirty miles."

"Near the nude beach."

"How do you know about that?"

"Doesn't everyone know where that beach is?"

"No. Only nudists or voyeurs do. Which one are you? What I want to know is how'd you hear about the burning?"

"My wife has a scanner."

"Thanks, I'll call for the report. Quite a shiner there."

Snickers were heard throughout the room. "He was taken down by a couple of teens," someone shouted. "Heard they won," was shouted from the other side of the room.

"It was more than two," said Smith lamely. "If I acted the way these brats act, my daddy would have whooped me."

"All it took was a few kids to give you a whooping," was the reply shouted from across the room. Smith blushed and left the room.

A couple of kids would be able to take me down these days, thought Edie, *with no problem.* She vowed to step up her workout routine. The phone startled Edie out of her funk. It was Fred; he'd just heard from Mrs. Washington. She reported that her husband was visiting a friend while she was out of the country. She gave a name, Jake Thomas, and Fred found the address. Would tomorrow be soon enough for an interview he asked? *Today would have been better*, Edie thought, *but I'll take what I can get.* They arranged to meet at nine the next morning. Edie would drive. With her schedule, it gave her more flexibility, and she'd have all the baby stuff with her, in case of an emergency. There wasn't anything else for Edie to do. She went home. Smiling. Something was happening. Relief had finally come.

12

*

F red was leaning against the building waiting for Edie. Edie was double-parked, leaning on the horn. Fred finally looked in her direction.

"I was looking for you in the lot. You know it's illegal to double-park?" said Fred, leaning in through the window after he had finally realized who the obnoxious driver was.

"So write me a ticket. Get in. You're wasting daylight and holding up traffic," said Edie as drivers lined up behind her and pounded on their car horns, as if that would get Edie moving. Fred opened the car door, stretched, and then slowly folded himself into the car. "Are you trying to get me a ticket?" she asked.

"Wanted to listen as you educated the cop who was bold enough to give you some advice about parking . . . let alone a ticket."

"Provocateur. The cops know my car, they try to stay away."

"That's what we've been telling you, trouble seems to come looking for you, and everyone else stays away."

"But you."

"My lucky day."

"So, where are we going and what can you tell me about this guy—this friend of Washington's?"

"We're going to Vilas."

"Damn, I should have brought my kid."

"The street, not the zoo. We are seeing a Jake Thomas who has graciously consented to talk with us at nine forty-five. He's a computer consultant. No records that I can find."

"Not even a parking ticket?"

"Nothing."

"Clean? Must be a model citizen. Who does he work for?"

"He's a freelancer. I'm assuming he works for small companies who can't afford their own IT person."

"Is he any good?"

"Haven't seen any testimonials, but he does live on Vilas—that should tell you something."

"Just wondering if he'd be available to work for Phil."

"Ask him on your own time."

Edie took Doty to Martin Luther King Boulevard meandering through the streets of Madison as she hugged the shores of Lake Monona before turning onto Vilas Avenue. Vilas, an older neighborhood of Madison, well-kept houses and gardens, across from the zoo, which was near the shores of Lake Wingra, and on another side of the lake—the Arboretum. There was an understated sense of elegance to the area, grace from a time when those were valued. This was a beautiful part of Madison. It was one of the areas she, and thousands of other Madisonians, would love to live in when their ship came in and a house became available. It would never happen, she knew.

"You could have taken a shorter route," said Fred as he got out of the car.

"Yeah, but I don't get to see any of the lakes or Madison from where I live. I miss them."

Edie looked over the houses. They were well–kept properties that were across from the zoo and Lake Wingra. Not much traffic except on weekends. Prime city location. Yes, she could live here, even with the weekend traffic jams. She'd just have to convince Phil that he could give up country living. He could come to love living in the city with neighbors on every side. And, if he sold his business, they could afford a house on Vilas Avenue. Good luck with that, Edie thought. If they ever moved to this street, she'd have to take a second job— hopefully one that wouldn't land her in jail. Yeah, right, she thought, as if Phil would ever part with country living. Edie knew she'd never live on this or any Madison street as long as she stayed with Phil, but at least today she was being invited into one of those houses.

Fred pushed the doorbell twice before they heard footsteps. A thin man opened the door. Edie guessed him to be about six foot, slim—possibly a runner, maybe biker—thinning brown hair, sculpted face, straight nose, lips sliding toward non-existence. Edie wondered if men ever got lip augmentation to help hide their age. Yet Jake Thomas had a smile that held your attention, brown eyes that took in everything. He was somewhere around mid– forties, and had an excellent taste in clothing. Edie liked a well-dressed man. "I'm Fred Price, FBI. My partner and I have an appointment with Jake Thomas."

"That's me, I've been expecting you," Jake said as he opened the door wider.

"I'm Edie Swift, Dane County detective." She added a weak handshake to her list of observations about Jake Thomas.

"If you don't mind, we'll meet in the back. Follow me, please," said Jake.

He took them past the living room, which had Oriental rugs scattered across the highly polished maple floor. Edie noted the sparsely furnished rooms, meant to display each piece of furniture, she guessed. Yet each piece was exquisite, and probably expensive, but somehow it looked homey, and comfortable. She thought of her own home, a catchall of his and her furniture when she and Phil decided to live together. Maybe, when there was time and money and no babies, they could afford this level of luxury. Edie sighed. "Lovely home."

"All my wife's doing. She told me that when she was a little girl she had always dreamed of living here. Lucky me, I got to make her dream come true," said Jake as he led them through a spotless kitchen to a back room. The view was breathtaking, right out of one of those beautiful home magazines she was always eyeing when waiting in line at the grocery store.

"Gorgeous garden," said Edie, taking a chair opposite the windows so she could gaze at the garden during the interview. If Phil hired this guy to do his computer stuff, maybe she could hire his wife to create a garden for her. One more reason for her to go back to work . . . hire a gardener. Fred sat to one side of Edie, Jake Thomas across from her.

"Again, my wife gets all the credit," said Jake, watching Edie become absorbed in the splendor. "This is my favorite room of the house. I work here often. I'm surprised I get any work done back here. My wife landscaped this area so that there was something to capture and please the eye in each season. Remarkable, isn't it? After our conversation, I would be happy to show you the rest of the house."

It took a moment for Edie to wrestle with her work ethic, but she finally declined the offer, with qualifications. "Sorry, but I can't do that at this time. I'm on duty and Agent Price, who rode with me, needs to get back to his office."

Fred led off with the questions, as it was obvious that Edie had forgotten the mission. It seemed as if motherhood had changed her. "We've been informed that you were a friend of Russell Washington."

"Were? Has something happened to him?"

"Didn't Mrs. Washington call you?"

"Last thing Russell told me was that she was in Africa."

"She is on her way back."

"Why? What has happened?"

"At this time, we're not at liberty to say," said Edie, her attention still on the garden.

Mr. Thomas gasped; a manicured hand flew to his mouth. "Is he the man found at Indian Lake?"

"Can't say, we're waiting for a positive ID," said Edie, turning her attention from the garden to Jake Thomas. "For now, we'd like to hear what you know about Russell Washington; what he was doing here and why."

"Russell and I are—were—are friends. I don't know what to say. He came for a visit. He'd been promising to come for the last ten years, but was only able to arrange it now while his wife was in Africa."

"What did you two do?" asked Edie.

"Mostly caught up on our lives, talked about old times. We visited some Madison sights."

"Such as?" asked Fred.

"The Capitol, the Saturday farmer's market downtown, the university, the Union Terrace, we did State Street."

"State Street?" quizzed Edie. "Reliving your college years?"

"We were not students at Madison, detective. Russell wanted to see the university we had heard so much about when we were students. It was known for its academic rigor, but also its history of endless anti-war riots, the massive Halloween bacchanal. The university was always rumored to be the top party school in the nation, but first you had to make the academic cut. And State Street is part of that experience, ask any alumnus." Jake Thomas paused, staring at his hands; he pushed back the cuticle on his left finger. He took a deep breath, looked up, and continued. "I don't know what will be of use to you. But, to start, we first met at college. Like any reunion of old friends we talked of old times, caught up on what we are doing now."

"When did you last see him?" asked Fred.

"Last Saturday. We went to the game. We did a pub crawl on State Street. Ate. Drank a few more beers. Wondered if we ever looked as young as the students around us did. We agreed that we were probably just as arrogant as they are, and maybe a little stupider than them. Drank some more beer and started talking about our aches and pains."

"What time did you leave?" asked Edie.

"About ten. I'm getting older, can't handle the hours and beer like I could."

"So you went home?" asked Fred.

"Yes."

"And what did Mr. Washington do?"

"Stayed at the bar. Beyond that, I couldn't say."

"What bar did you leave him at?"

"Sorry, but I don't remember the bar's name, it was near Francis Street."

"Did you hear from him after that?"

"No."

"Didn't you think it was strange that he didn't contact you?"

"No. I did offer him a ride to the airport, but he declined. We said our good-byes and then I left."

"There were no messages that he got home all right?" asked Edie.

"No. Didn't expect any. He's a big boy; he can take care of himself. Thought he might shoot me an e-mail or text when he got home or a written note when Georgie got home, she's a stickler for etiquette. But, no, I wasn't concerned about it."

Edie watched as Fred continued to question Jake Thomas. *Damn,* she thought, *this case will be solved the old-fashioned way—pounding the pavement until it starts to crack open.* She watched as Jake smoothly answered Fred's questions, no hesitation, no pause to think. He could be one of those slick defense lawyers, if he wanted to, she thought. Wrapped up in her observations, it took a few seconds for her to realize that Fred was shaking Jake's hand. She rose, shook Jake's hand—*wimpy* again sprang to mind, nothing else about the man would lead to that conclusion. Edie followed them out, "I am surprised that it's quiet here. I thought with the zoo across the road it would be loud."

"The trees and brush obstruct the noise. When it gets unbearable, we escape to the lake house. Is there anything else I can answer?" asked Jake.

"Not at the moment," said Fred. "Thank you. Please, call either of us, if you can think of anything . . . anything at all." He handed Jake his business card.

Edie, too, handed her business card to Jake.

With the car doors shut and the engine idling, Fred began to talk, "What's your assessment?"

"He's smooth," said Edie. "And I'm in the wrong business. He owns a house like that and a lake house. I should've gotten a tour today—I'd like to see what is in that garage."

"I know that good IT people can make a bundle. But we know nothing else about his life. We don't know what his wife does. Maybe their parents left them a bundle. We don't know, because we don't need to know. But I agree, there's something about him."

"Anything in particular?" asked Edie.

"Lots of things, his smoothness . . . more slickness than smooth."

"Maybe he missed his calling, should've been a defense lawyer, he's slick enough."

"Yes. With many people, you can almost see the brain kicking into gear, but not with him, his brain never went out of gear. Though he seemed to give thoughtful answers, they also seemed rehearsed. And he was constantly watching us for our reactions."

"I didn't like his handshake . . . wimpy."

"Everyone's is wimpy compared to you. Where are you going next?"

"To the office, gotta write up today's report before picking up Hillary."

"You don't have to pump?"

"Yeah, I need to do that. Maybe I'll go into the office, write and pump at the same time. The guys would love that."

"I think you like making them uncomfortable."

"They see blood and gore, the dregs of society, the gory mess of passion, but a woman nursing her baby makes them squeamish? Go figure. Let's get this day finished."

But first, Edie took a different scenic route back to downtown Madison.

13

*

Edie dropped Fred off at his car. She did write up the morning's interview. She sat at her desk and pumped, although Edie made sure the pump and breast were under wraps. The deputies who stayed in the office quickly took a coffee break, or tried to avert their eyes.

When Edie finished the report, she looked at her watch. She had some time before picking up her daughter, since Hillary was with Aunt Jill. Her aunt probably wouldn't mind. After all, she'd known Edie for a long time and understood Edie's dedication to work. Edie decided to spend the time at Indian Lake.

Edie drove around Indian Lake clockwise, then counterclockwise; she wanted to see the place from as many angles as she could. On the backside of the park she pulled off the road. Sitting still in the quiet of autumn might help to focus.

"Okay, where am I with the case? Fact, Russell Washington came to visit his friend Jake Thomas. How do I know that? Jake Thomas said during our interview. What was Washington doing while in Madison? Catching up on old times with a college friend and visiting the Madison sites, per Jake Thomas. Was Washington doing anything out of character? He was clean and straight, according to Kirsten Sather from The Morning Rose. Jake Thomas didn't know of anything, at least that he would admit to. Tox screen isn't back yet. I'll have to wait for Mrs. Washington to arrive to know anymore. So where am I? In the middle of nowhere. Nowhere nearer the end than when I began. Empty-handed except for a dead man. All I can do is wait. I hate waiting. I gotta make something happen, NOW," Edie shouted. At the edge of her peripheral vision she caught a flash of red.

A red pickup truck stopping in the field across from her pulled Edie from her rant. She watched as a man snapped on a tool belt, took a ladder from the truck bed, set it up against an oak tree, climbed the ladder, and began pounding something into the tree. Edie got out of her car, crammed the car keys deep into her pocket, double-checked that they were there, and then went to talk with the man on the ladder.

"Excuse me, sir. I'm Detective Edie Swift with Dane County Sheriff," she yelled up to the man.

"Good for you. I'm Jerome Adler. Farmer. Can I see your ID?"

Edie walked back to her car, pulled the badge and ID from the diaper bag. She grabbed a few business cards and a pen, just in case. Another thing she'd have to work on, a place to put her work stuff until her boobs went back to normal size and she could wear a jacket with pockets.

"Was wondering what you're doing?" Edie asked when she returned and held up her ID for Farmer Adler to see.

"Taking care of my property. Any law against that?" replied Mr. Adler, as he pounded in nails to hold a camera.

This was one of the times Edie wished she were a flight attendant so she could charge the guy with obstruction. "No."

"Then what are you doing on my property?"

"Investigating the crime that happened at Indian Lake last week."

"Heard about it. Don't know nothing about it," he said, climbing down the ladder.

"That your field over there?"

"No, it belongs to Karl Boehnen."

"Where does he live?"

"Over on Schuman Road."

"Can you spell the last name for me?" asked Edie flipping over a business card to record the information.

"B–O–E–H–N–E–N. If you're going to talk to him, tell him to get his kid's muffler fixed. I need my sleep."

"Thanks, I'll do that. What's he doing to wreck your sleep?"

"He's driving all over the country without a muffler. Got my missus mad at me. She said I could hear that car, but claims that I never hear what she says to me."

"Oh . . . what are you nailing to the tree?"

"Trail camera. Want to catch the sons–of–bitches that are shooting my deer on my land and leaving them to rot. I don't know what people are thinking these days, they must never have been hungry."

"Love to see the film when you get something." Edie handed him one of her business cards. "If you can't reach me directly, leave a message with our main line. They'll know how to get in touch with me."

Jerome Adler looked at the card then stuffed it into his wallet. "Say, what have you found out about that man in the park?"

"Not much, yet."

"You guys aren't fast workers, are you? Those TV shows could teach you a few things."

"Depends, the park had to be combed for clues—that takes a while. And you know that TV is scripted, don't you?"

"Yes, I'm just yanking your chain. Hope you catch whoever did it, my wife and the whole neighborhood are jumpy. Everyone is looking over their shoulders these days. And locking doors on every one of their buildings. It's a pain when you're trying to finish combining and have to unlock every door just to get a screwdriver."

"We'll do our best. Call me if you get any hits on the camera or if you hear anything. Thanks."

Edie and Jerome Adler shook hands. She took one last look around. Most of the trees had dropped their leaves. First snow isn't too far off, she thought. She went to her car and headed back to Madison.

Aunt Jill's house was chilly. Edie thought her aunt might be on one of her environmental kicks. Save energy for future generations; if you're cold, put on a sweater, was the mantra heard while growing up. Then the thought occurred that maybe Aunt Jill couldn't afford to pay the heating bill, she was getting old. She'd have to figure a way to slip some money to Aunt Jill, maybe pad her babysitting payment. Leave money on the kitchen counter for Aunt Jill to find. Add money to Aunt Jill's birthday, mother's day, and Christmas presents. But seeing Aunt Jill, Edie understood.

The cold was coming from Aunt Jill. Many people fumed when angry, Aunt Jill went cold. Edie agreed with Robert Frost that when the world's end came she'd rather have the fire instead of the freeze. Edie flash-backed to the first time she had experienced Aunt Jill's freeze–out. Edie was thirteen and had come home, for the first time, at sunrise.

"The rules haven't changed," Aunt Jill said as she kissed Hillary before handing her over to Edie.

"I'm sorry." Edie remembered the steps to getting back into Aunt Jill's good graces.

"If you are late, you call. You may be an adult, but it still applies."

Edie thought she heard her aunt's voice crack. Saw her draw back her shoulders. *Oh, oh, what's coming next*, thought Edie.

"Thought you might be turning into your mother," said Aunt Jill when Edie entered the house. "I raised you better than that. If I have to I can raise another generation."

Edie was stunned. She never wanted to be compared to her mother. "I was working on my case."

"This little one is important, too."

"I am aware of that."

"Then call."

"But I'm not that late."

"An hour."

"I didn't think you'd mind."

"I do."

"You never did."

"Yes, I did. But that was when it was only me. You have a child to think about. And today I'm not the one you need to apologize to, you need to talk with Hillary."

"A baby?"

"Yes, she has been waiting for you."

"But I was working."

"Edie, pull on your big girl pants and figure out how to do both. Most of the rest of us did."

"Except my mother."

"That is a discussion for another time."

14

✳

Edie stood in the Dane County Regional Airport holding a sign with "Georgia Washington" written boldly on it. Since she was the lead on the Washington case not only was she assigned to interview Mrs. Washington, but also to guide her around Madison during her stay. Edie hoped that she looked presentable. During their brief phone conversation, Mrs. Washington was exact—not one word extra was used. From that interview, Edie surmised that Mrs. Washington was exacting. So Edie had cobbled together clothing she thought was presentable: a clean pullover T-shirt, a cardigan that fit pre-Hillary but now thrown on for the in-case moment of milk runs, and a pair of pregnancy pants—it was the best outfit she could put together, the one least like being pulled from a dumpster dive during Madison's annual Hippie Christmas, which was the August day when the university students moved to new apartments and dumped everything they didn't want to move. Edie had found a number of treasures during her dumpster diving days. Edie hoped that Mrs. Washington didn't judge a book solely by its cover. She held her sign higher as people flowed past security, hoping they saw it and not her clothes. And there Mrs. Washington was, impeccable. At least that lady fit the image Edie had of her.

It was her. Her hair looked as if Mrs. Washington had stepped out of a salon instead off a flight from Atlanta via Chicago. Her yellow suit was wrinkle–free and the lady was wearing high heels. *Who wears high heels on an airplane?* Edie thought. She pulled her cardigan tighter and wished for winter and a jacket that could hide the baby fat she still carried. Edie felt like a country bumpkin, nothing about her was quite right. She knew she could never pass Mrs. Washington's inspection; Edie didn't want to undergo that scrutiny and for a moment she thought of walking away. But she didn't. She held the sign higher. The woman Edie identified as Mrs. Washington approached her.

"I'm Mrs. Washington. It is a pleasant surprise to have someone greet me."

Edie watched as Mrs. Washington did a head–to–toe assessment of her. She had not passed the inspection. "I'm Detective Edith Swift of the Dane County Sheriff's Department. Do you have any luggage?"

"Only a carry–on."

Edie was relieved that they didn't have to wait for luggage. Now all she had to figure out was what to talk about on the way to the hotel. What do you say to a woman whose husband was recently murdered?

"How was your flight?" Edie led off with the old standby conversation opener.

"Which one?"

"How many transfers did you have to make to get here?"

"From Atlanta, two. I am glad that I don't have to fly through Chicago on a regular basis."

"One of the necessary evils when trying to get to Madison."

"My sympathies."

Edie searched for the next topic, nothing came to mind. A little history of the area usually filled the awkward gaps of silence.

"Well, this is Madison, the capital of Wisconsin. The Capitol building is said to be designed after the US Capitol. Madison is also the home of the University of Wisconsin-Madison, one of Lincoln's land-grant colleges and world-renowned. Go Badgers." Edie wasn't good at small talk. She jumped feet first into finding out about Mrs. Washington. "Why weren't you with him during the visit?"

"I was in Africa."

"Doing what?"

"Doing work at a school I help to support. And that charity work has nothing to do with my husband or his work. I've heard about this city," said Georgia Washington, matching Edie's directness. "Jake Thomas has been trying to get my husband to move here. I don't know why Russell would even think that this Southern girl would move to a cold climate. What are the winters up here really like?"

"Usually cold and snowy, but it's changing, like the rest of the world."

"I can't think what would possess people to spend their winters here. What is there to do here except freeze?"

"Winter has its own beauty. I can't imagine what people do during the scorching, sweltering Southern summers."

"Live with air-conditioning."

"We have central heat for our winters."

"I didn't think you huddled around a wood stove."

"Only during electrical outages."

The women went silent for the rest of the ride to The Morning Rose.

Edie pulled up to the hotel, handed Mrs. Washington her business card and arranged to pick her up the next morning at eight.

Edie was at the hotel at 7:59 a.m. Damn, Mrs. Washington was waiting on the porch and as impeccably dressed as she was yesterday. Mrs. Washington was on the sidewalk before Edie pulled up to the curb.

"Didn't think you'd remember my car," Edie said.

"When you're married to someone like Russell, you start to notice and remember everything. Glad to see you were on time. Hate those people who let the minutes slip away. Soon they find their life is nearing the end and they can't account for anything."

"True, but some allowance needs to be made for life changes and the bumps in the road."

"Says who?"

"Me," said Edie. "How was the hotel?"

"One of the best I have stayed at. My comfort was their goal. The service was impeccable and unobtrusive. The food is delicious."

There was no place to go with their conversation, it was caught between two brick walls. Edie pulled into a parking space and escorted Mrs. Washington into her office. Fred was waiting, Edie was relieved to see.

"Mrs. Washington, I'm Fred Price from the FBI."

"Please, call me Georgia," Mrs. Washington said with all the Southern charm that had been hidden from Edie. "It's nice to know that someone competent is working on Russell's case."

Fred suppressed a laugh. "Georgia, we talked before, but I'd like my colleague to hear it directly."

Georgia Washington did a quick head–to–toe assessment of Edie, again, gave a little shrug of acceptance, and sat in the chair that Fred held for her. Edie knew she hadn't passed muster and never would, but that didn't matter; what concerned Edie was the struggle with Georgia Washington over who would have the upper hand. Edie took a chair across from Georgia Washington and conceded that it might be a draw. Edie proceeded with the interview.

"Georgia," Edie noticed that Mrs. Washington looked irritated, "do you know why your husband was in Madison?"

"To visit his friend, Jacob Thomas."

"Why wasn't he with you?"

"Because he wanted to visit his friend . . . and I didn't. With my scheduled work in Kenya, Russell took the opportunity to come here."

"Why didn't you want to come?"

"Jacob Thomas."

"You don't like Jacob Thomas?"

"I've met the man a mere handful of times, and each time I come away disturbed. He has been friendly toward me, often going out of his way, but still I can't bring myself to like the man. He is Russell's friend, not mine."

"Did your husband talk about his work?"

"When it came to work, Russell knew when to keep his mouth shut. There was only superficial pillow talk concerning his work."

"Tell me about your husband. What was he like? What did he do with his leisure time?"

"What has that got to do with his murder?"

"I'm trying to get a picture of the man. It helps me to create a picture of what he may have done while he was here."

"Meticulous."

Not surprising, thought Edie, but whose obsession for order came first—Georgia Washington's or Russell's?

"Was he an alcoholic?"

"He limited his drinking to one cocktail on social occasions."

"He drank more at home?"

"None. His drinking was social. Why these questions?"

"Mr. Thomas said that he and Mr. Washington were bar-hopping."

"They were college friends. What memories they wanted to relive when they got together is beyond my knowledge."

Edie knew the answer to her next question, before she asked it, but she needed confirmation. "Did your husband ever have an affair?"

"No."

"Did you ever suspect him of having an affair?"

"Never. My husband loved me, and we both understood that there were only two people in our marriage—him and me. Excuse me, could you direct me to the restroom?"

"Down the hall to the right," said Edie.

Edie sat back in her chair, "Nothing soft about that woman, she's all edges."

"Excuse my political incorrectness, but look who's calling the kettle black," said Fred.

"I get the feeling that she thinks I'm a local yokel."

"When you are at the Washingtons' level, that attitude is endemic."

"Think there is anything more to learn about Russell?"

"No, unless you want their family history."

"Which is what?"

"Upstanding overachievers."

Edie stood when Mrs. Washington entered the room. She extended her hand, "Mrs. Washington, thank you for your time and information. It has given me some insight into your husband. My deepest condolences to you and your family on the loss of Russell."

Georgia took her hand, "Thank you. Where do I go from here? I'd like to see my husband's body."

Firm handshake, thought Edie. "It isn't a pretty sight."

"Death is never pretty," Georgia said.

"Fred has agreed to guide you through the rest of your time here."

Fred had agreed to no such thing, but he ushered Georgia Washington out of the room and through the endless arrangements needed to return Russell Washington's body to Atlanta and the people who had loved him.

Edie locked the door behind them. She wanted to pump and think, not listen to the office gossip. She placed the pumps on her breast and thought about Jake Thomas and the people who didn't like him.

15

✳

Mrs. Voss knocked on the front door before opening it and calling out. "Anybody home?"

"In the kitchen," yelled Edie. "Come on back."

"Just came to see how the little one is doing."

"Fine," said Edie placing the pump parts on the rack to dry. "You?"

"A little stiff this morning. The older I get, the better I understand my grandmother. She always said her bones told her the weather sooner and better than any weatherman."

"What are your bones predicting?"

"Storm coming in a few days. How's the case coming?"

"Plodding along. Nothing new. I'll be interviewing people tonight. Maybe get a few leads."

"Who's watching Hillary?"

"Phil."

"Phil!"

"Yes, her daddy."

"How did you get a German man to watch his own kid?"

"Didn't give him a choice, it's part of parenting. And he's not German, he's an American."

"Wish I'd married someone with his attitude."

"Phil and I aren't married."

"I was born too early."

Mrs. Voss watched Edie put things in their place then proceed to rummage through cupboards and the fridge. "Are you looking for something special? Maybe I can help."

"Something Phil can open for supper."

"He doesn't cook?"

"Didn't have to. His mother cooked or he popped a frozen pizza into the oven, or called for delivery. When I first knew Phil, he must've had more than twenty take-out menus taped to his kitchen wall. The numbers not on his speed dial, he had memorized."

"I'm planning on meatloaf tonight. I could bring over a plate for him."

"Would you? He'd appreciate that." Edie opened the freezer wider to show Mrs. Voss. "Because I don't have any frozen pizzas."

"My pleasure. Be nice to cook for someone other than me. Should I bring extra for you?"

"No, thank you. I'm eating in Madison tonight."

"What are you doing there?"

"Looking for a cookbook for Phil, it's time he learned."

"Oh, I was going to guess it was about your case. Making any progress?"

"Some. And that is all I can give out," Edie smiled at such an expert and yet seemingly innocent interrogation. "Is there something I can do for you?"

"No, just stopped over for a bit of conversation."

"Usually I'd love to talk, but since I'm gone tonight, I need some rest. Thanks for the food. When can I tell Phil you'll stop over?"

"Six too early?"

"Usually, but I'll tell Phil to be home early," said Edie, as she walked to the front door with Mrs. Voss. Edie stood at the door until she saw Mrs. Voss safely enter her own house. Then Edie locked the door and went to take a nap.

Before heading to Madison, Edie double-checked the in-case-of-trouble list that she had: paper, pencil, and a photo of Russell Washington. She was ready.

Phil sat on the couch watching, "Aren't you forgetting something?"

"Oh, yeah. Thanks," Edie kissed Hillary then Phil good-bye.

"I'm glad your priorities are straight, but what about the pump, your gun, and your cell?"

"I will need the pump, but I'd like to be as inconspicuous as possible."

"You're a mom. How many college kids take a second look at mothers?"

"True. Never thought I'd be tied to a breast pump," Edie said, as she went to the kitchen to assemble the pump.

"That was never in my fantasies either."

Edie returned, zipping up the pump bag as she headed for the door.

"Where's your gun?"

"Shouldn't need it."

"You're on duty. You may not need it, but what if another cop needs your assistance?"

Edie sighed as she went to the bedroom to get her gun out of the locked box on the highest shelf of the closet where she kept it. Now she was ready. She was almost out the front door when Phil came out of the kitchen.

"What about your cell?"

"It's charging. Why don't you just come with me?"

"I'm on babysitting duty."

"You two could sit at the Union."

"No thanks. I'd be bothered all night by young coeds trying to pick me up by adoring my baby. I'll sit here and bond with Hillary. Use my cell." Phil tossed her the cell. "Your loss." Edie hesitated, Phil didn't stop her. She was good to go.

Edie was still formulating her plan when she parked at the Lake Street Ramp. She hadn't been on State Street in years. With work, hooking up with Phil, and now the baby, there was no longer a reason for her to cruise the street. She wondered how much it had changed and where she should start. She felt something warm trickle down her chest. First place, the Union, she knew of a place there where she could pump.

The Union was pretty much as she had left it the year she graduated, too many years ago, thought Edie, while she waited for the elevator. She saw students gathered around the candy store, more at the ice cream stand— drooling as they tried to decide if they should indulge in their favorite flavor or not. The ones who walked away had checked their pockets and come up short, the others indulged. No changes there, different faces, but kids were still kids. Edie noted that most of them seemed too young to be there. Were they really too young or had she slipped over an unknown divide when she turned thirty last year?

Edie stepped out of the elevator onto the fourth floor, her breast pump slung over her shoulder, and walked to the ladies' lounge. It wasn't there. Damn. When did that happen? It was the one thing she had used every day. It had been her place to get away from the noise of the libraries. She couldn't afford to live on campus, so she had made the ladies' lounge her home away from home—a place to stretch out and rest. Now, it was gone. Damn, someone picked the wrong thing to change. Edie went in search of an empty room to pump in.

Plans for the night were congealing until The Bookstore caught her eye. Good place to look for Phil's cookbook. Edie walked in, promising herself that she was there only for Phil's present.

"Where are the books?" she said out loud. Edie looked around to see if anyone was nearby who might be able to answer that question. The barista at a newly in-stalled coffee bar shrugged her shoulders and continued to wipe down the counter in an effort to look busy.

The first floor of The Bookstore had been taken over by clothes. The basement, where class books were shelved, once held wall-to-wall books and students in her time. But the students weren't there and the books had dwindled to a few. Sad, Edie thought, remembering how she'd browse the shelves to see what books she had to read, what books she would like to read, and what classes she should take the next semester. She shrugged her shoulders, things change, and then scoured the store for a cookbook. Edie found one, almost shouting her thanks to the students who never bothered to learn to cook before they left home.

Paging through the cookbook, Edie acknowledged her hunger pains. She went in search of a decent meal, not student food; her stomach couldn't handle the gut bombs any more. She knew what she didn't want: pizza, brats, hamburgers, subs. That narrowed the choices considerably. Most of the lower State Street restaurants catered to students who had limited time, money, and uneducated palates. One of the Mediterranean restaurants was closed. The other had a long line. The last remaining Italian restaurant took her name and number; they'd call her when a table opened. Edie left the restaurant trying to remember where a decent coffee place was. A place where she could sit in the window and watch the passing parade while she drank decaf tea and waited for the restaurant to call her.

She found one of a few coffee places on State Street that fit the bill. Edie claimed a window table by placing her bag on a chair; there it was less likely to develop legs. And put her book on the table. She hoped that it would still be there after she ordered.

It was. She came back with a pot of hot water, a teabag of decaf Darjeeling and a madeleine cookie—she was hungry. Edie dropped the teabag into the pot before turning her attention to the street.

Edie wondered if the students were hunkering down for exam week, or maybe researching their term papers, or, more likely, afraid to come out in the cold. But still, she saw a few less hearty souls already bundled in winter coats, braving the winds that blew down State Street. She tried to imagine what they would do when the temperature dropped and the wind took over State Street. Edie sipped her tea and watched and asked herself which person on the street saw something different about Russell Washington on Saturday night, and which of them would step out of their comfort zone to admit it?

A person from the next table tapping on her shoulder brought her back to reality, "Excuse me, excuse me, ma'am, your phone is ringing."

Edie pulled the annoying thing from her pocket, "Hello...Phil, is Hillary okay? What? What table is ready?...Sorry, I forgot I had your phone...Gave the restaurant my number...Yeah, I'm okay, just deep in thought...Thanks." She flipped the cell shut, put on her coat, and headed for the restaurant.

It took her a moment to realize that someone was shouting for her, "Ma'am, ma'am." When had she changed from a miss to a ma'am? Edie turned around, a man with a winter coat thrown over his apron was walking toward her carrying her pump bag and her book. "The table next to you said you forgot this." She took her belongings, thanked him, and then finished her walk to the restaurant.

Edie ordered the house special chef salad with the house dressing. Her meal was exactly as she remembered, delicious. Or, maybe it was delicious because she didn't have to make it. Anyway, she was hungry and the food was marvelous.

It was only when the waitress was clearing the table that Edie remembered to show her Washington's picture. No, the waitress hadn't seen him, but then she tried to avoid working weekends—she'd make great tips, but too many drunks for her to deal with. Maybe if she came back tomorrow or Saturday night the regular weekenders should be on. After paying the bill, Edie pushed away from the table to continue her quest.

It was the same at every bar she stopped at. Sorry, the regular weekenders wouldn't be on till tomorrow, some not until Saturday. Edie meandered up State Street, stopping at the bars and restaurants. The closer she got to the Capitol, the fewer people who were on the street and fewer stores were open. An inhospitable feeling swirled around the buildings. Edie knew that she could talk her way out of any situation, and fight if she had to, but walking that part of State she was glad that Phil had insisted that she take her gun.

Edie, for old times' sake, detoured to The Burger Joint on Henry. The place was crowded. Students were elbow–to–elbow in the booths, around the pool tables, the pinball machines, and the electronic games. She smiled. It was exactly the way she remembered it, for this joint, during her time on campus, had been her home away from home. It was odd because the students from the boonies, and the students from the inner cities both said it reminded them of home. And for all the other students, it was a taste of living on the edge.

A waitress was sipping a pop when Edie pushed through the crowd and shouted in her ear, "Excuse me."

The waitress put on a smile and turned toward Edie. "Can I help you?"

"Yes, I'm Detective Swift, and I'm looking for someone who worked last Saturday night."

"That would be me."

Edie pulled the picture of Washington from the pump bag. "Did you see this man last Saturday?"

The waitress took the photo from Edie, and then handed it back—quickly. "Do you see the crowd in here? Last Saturday was a football Saturday. On football Saturdays, it's worse. If a person isn't one of my regular customers or does something stupid, I wouldn't remember. I don't have time to people watch."

"He might have been here with a white man."

"That certainly narrows it down."

"Who else worked on Saturday?"

"Nola and Tia."

"Are they here tonight?"

"Yeah, they should be up shortly, their orders are ready."

Edie turned to people–watch. Two young women were walking toward the bar; the blonde's hair was pulled back in a ponytail which kept rhythm with her walk. The brunette's hair cascaded down her back, a few strands creeping over her shoulder, which she swept back with her hand. Both were wearing impossibly tight jeans and shirts that opened to their navels, revealing sports bras. Tits and ass, thought Edie, it never changes. To get into the university those girls were probably brilliant, but tits and ass were all that anyone responded to. Probably got great tips too. Which probably paid their tuition. Edie sighed over the eternal exchange of money for looks.

"Tia, Nola, this is Detective Swift," said Mallory, the jack-of-all-trades at The Burger Joint, interrupting Edie's thoughts.

Edie shoved Washington's picture at them as the girls reviewed the orders.

"Be back in a sec," said the blonde as she hefted a full tray to her shoulder.

The brunette peeked at the picture, and then took her tray with a promise to return.

Both girls came back. "Let me see that picture again," said the brunette who had introduced herself as Nola. "Don't remember the face."

The blonde introduced herself as Tia. "I don't either. What did he do?" she asked handing the picture back to Edie.

"Got himself killed," said Edie.

"You think he was in here?" said Tia.

"Possibly."

"Hey, is that the guy in the paper?" asked Nola.

"Yes," replied Edie.

Both girls buttoned their shirts so that only a hint of their sports bra showed.

"Sorry, I can't help you. That Saturday was extra busy," said Tia.

Edie handed each of the waitresses her business card. "Maybe you can ask around, see if someone remembers this guy. Call me at this number, if you come up with something." Edie made her way through the crowd to fresh air and State Street.

Nothing. She had come up with nothing. What a waste of time. Then she remembered Phil's present. The night wasn't a total loss, maybe she should give him the present early. She could use a night off from cooking.

Phil had left the lights on for her. Edie checked on Hillary before going into her own bedroom. She dropped her clothes at the bedside, she was too tired to do more, and snuggled against Phil.

"You're cold," said Phil when Edie put her feet against his shins.

"You're warm. You didn't remind me to wear my wool socks."

"Can't think of everything," he said turning over and putting his arms around Edie. "Make any progress?"

"No. Made a few contacts. They all said the same thing, 'come back tomorrow.' Want to come with next time?"

"No, thanks. I like bonding with my daughter. Turn around so I can warm the other side."

Edie turned over. "How was your night?"

Phil pulled her closer. "Good. Mrs. Voss brought over a delicious meal, dessert included. She changed Hillary's poopy diaper, gave her a bottle, and rocked her to sleep."

"Did you do anything?"

"Ate and enjoyed getting to know our neighbor. And told my mother to mind her own business about us getting married."

"You have potential," murmured Edie, as she fell asleep in Phil's warm arms.

Phil listened for her slowing breaths. When Edie was safely asleep, he whispered in her ear, "When are we getting married?"

16

✳

It was a good morning, Edie was trying to psych herself up. The previous night had done nothing but remind her that she was aging. Ma'am . . . how could anyone mistake her for a ma'am? She pulled her T-shirt up, looked at her nursing bra, and readjusted the pads that had slipped out of place. She let the T-shirt flop back into place. Maybe that guy was right, she was a ma'am. Edie returned to the task of plotting her day.

Pack up Hillary, drop her off at Aunt Jill, get car from the department, and interview farmer Boehnen. Exchange cars, pick up Hillary, on time. Pick up supper. Go home. Her life was becoming predictable, and her baby had become its center.

Edie knocked on farmer Boehnen's door. No answer. She looked for a doorbell, none. She knocked again, same result. Edie looked at the buildings: a shed, grain bins, and a barn with cows in its yard. Edie chose the barn as the most likely place this farmer would be in the morning.

She stepped into the barn, where a woman was scraping down the alley. "Excuse me," Edie said loudly, but not loud enough. Edie found the radio and turned it off. The woman turned around. "I'm looking for Mr. Boehnen."

"He's out combining. I'm Patricia Boehnen, his wife. Can I help you?"

"I'm Detective Edie Swift. Mind if I ask you a few questions about an incident at Indian Lake?"

"I talked to some other deputies, but as long as you can walk and talk at the same time, I'll answer them again. Sorry about that, but I'm the only one working this morning, so I can't stop and talk."

Edie kept pace with Patricia Boehnen as she scraped the barn's center alley. "I've read your statements given to the other deputies, just want to see if anything has jogged your memory since then."

"Sorry, haven't given it any thought." Patricia Boehnen stopped for a moment. "That's not quite true. I lock my doors, keep my cell nearby, and am thinking of buying a handgun. Other than that, I don't think about it." She continued with her chores.

"Anything out of the ordinary happen that night?"

"No. Normally, it's quiet in these parts, except during planting and harvest."

"Nothing out of the ordinary going on in the neighborhood?"

"Not that I've heard of."

Edie didn't know what to make of Patricia Boehnen. Was she hiding something, ignoring something, or refusing to acknowledge the world around her? "Hear your son has problems with his car's muffler."

"Tell my nosy neighbors to mind their own business. Karl said he'd fix Ian's car when harvest was done."

"Your son's name is Ian?"

"Yes."

"How old is he?"

"Sixteen."

"Has he said anything about that Saturday?"

"No, but then he wouldn't. He's still in the middle of teenage angst. I apologize a lot to my parents these days."

"Why is that?"

"Because as good a kid as Ian is, he's annoying and pushes the boundaries. Like any kid, like I probably did at his age."

Edie looked around the barn, trying to imagine how any farm kid had time to push boundaries. They pushed brooms, manure, hay, straw ... but not boundaries—they were too busy.

"Just moved to the country myself. I've been wondering what country kids do for entertainment."

"Pretty much what other kids their age do, mostly drive around when they're finished with their chores."

"What type of chores?"

"Depends on the farm. We have a dairy, so Ian helps with milking and chores. During the summer, he bales hay, straw. During the fall, he does whatever needs to be done."

"Doesn't sound typical for most teens these days."

"Maybe it should be," said Patricia Boehnen, scraping the last of the alley.

"Has Ian or Mr. Boehnen said anything about last Saturday?

"No. The only thing my husband and I talk about during harvest is the harvest ... and the weather. As for Ian, he's like most teens, I guess—they keep conversations with their parents short." Mrs. Boehnen had put the scraper away and picked up a broom and swept the outside alleys.

"What were you three doing that Saturday?"

"I milked, made supper. Karl was combining, came in early, slept. Ian helped me milk, and then went to the game and out with his friends."

"When will your husband and son be around? I'd like to talk to them."

"Best time for Karl is after harvest is done."

"Not an option. I need to talk to him within the next few days."

"Guess you could ride with while he's combining."

"Never been in a combine, worth a try. What about Ian?"

"With school and stuff, I can't give you an exact time. Why do you want to talk to him?"

"I'm talking to anyone and everyone who might have been in the area concerning last Saturday."

"The best time to catch Ian is at school."

"Do I have your permission to talk to him?"

"Yes, he doesn't have anything to hide." Patricia put the broom back in its place and went to the milk house. Edie followed.

"Could I talk to him today?"

"If you have to."

"Do you want to be there?"

"I don't think that's necessary. He's not going to say anything different from what he told the other deputies."

"Thanks. I'll stop by the school to talk with Ian, and then call you later today to give you an update on the conversation and set a time to talk with your husband."

17

✳

Edie was buzzed into Victor Berger High School and met at the front doors by the principal. Edie had forgotten how loud high school was; classes must have let out. Maybe it was a release from keeping their mouths shut while an adult talked that made the teens shout when released from class. Maybe it was the combination of hundreds of teens scurrying to lockers and their next class and the need to hear their own voices. Whatever the reason, it was loud.

She stood with the principal as kids moved from one classroom to another, some slammed their lockers, and others called to their friends down the hall. Edie caught bits of kids' plans for the weekend, none of which included studying. A bell rang. The hallways emptied, fast. The school was quiet. Edie followed the principal to her office.

The principal offered Edie a seat by the window, and then sat behind her desk. "Excuse me for not introducing myself earlier; it's hard to hear anything in the halls. I'm Principal Zander. What can I do for you?"

"I'm Detective Edie Swift, and I'd like to talk with Ian Boehnen."

Principal Zander called for Ian Boehnen's file, rapidly reviewing it after a counselor handed it to her. "Good kid, hasn't been in any trouble in school. What's this about?"

"I'm investigating the murder that occurred at the park."

"You think he was involved?"

"No, but he lives near there. He may have heard or seen something that could be useful to us. I arranged with his mother earlier to talk with Ian. She gave me verbal permission to talk to him."

"I'll have to confirm that," said Principal Zander, dialing the phone.

Edie looked around the room while listening to the one-sided phone conversation. She had no idea what a principal's office looked like—she always narrowly escaped from intimately knowing one. But then her high school had been huge; there were layers of bureaucracy before reaching the principal's office—and she had never been sent to any of them, either. The room was large, sparsely decorated, with lots of windows. Diplomas attesting to Principal Zander's education hung right behind her desk. Edie noticed the principal could be addressed as Dr. Zander. Edie was impressed and wondered how many students and their parents were cowed by the diplomas.

Principal Zander hung up the phone and dialed again. "Excuse me; I need to make a few more calls before I can help you."

Edie went back to looking around the room. Photos of all the classes that graduated under Principal Zander's administration hung on the wall, side-by-side with a few school awards. A few bookcases held professional books and journals. There was nothing personal in the room, except the diplomas. Edie wondered if the office's minimalism was deliberate. It could be effective in focusing the perpetrator's attention on the crime, or not. If Zander cozied-up the room, it could fool the perpetrator into thinking they were at home and make the kid bawl like a baby. Either could work. Edie made a mental note to talk to Zander about this, but not today.

Edie returned her attention to Principal Zander when she heard the phone returned to the cradle.

"I've talked to Mrs. Boehnen; she's confirmed that she did give you permission to talk to Ian. Next I talked to our superintendent. I'll be writing a report of what is discussed here. I, obviously, will be present during the time you are with Ian. He should be here in a moment." She set a chair next to Edie's, and then opened another window. "Might as well enjoy the last few nice days before winter sets in."

They waited for Ian, silent. Edie began to feel like a school kid waiting for some punishment, and she had done nothing wrong. At least nothing that should interest a school principal.

It was a relief to see Ian Boehnen standing in the doorway. Edie guessed that he, too, had never been called to a principal's office before.

"Come in, Ian, and have a seat."

Ian sat in the chair near Edie, and then moved it a few inches away from her.

"Ian, this is Detective Edie Swift. She has some questions about the Saturday before last. I've just talked with your mother; she has given permission for this conversation. As you are underage and this is happening during school hours, I will be present. I will also write an official report that will be read by the superintendent and put in your file. Do you understand me so far?"

Ian nodded.

"Ian, I need a verbal confirmation that you under-stand me."

"Yes," said Ian softly.

Edie was bored to death. *Let me get on with this interview*, she said silently.

"This has nothing to do with academic or other school performance, so this report will not be part of your official record. I expect that Detective Swift will send me a copy of her report concerning this conversation."

Edie nodded, of course, *but please be done with all this legal crap*, she silently pleaded.

"You may begin, Detective Swift."

"Thank you, Principal Zander. Ian, do you know that there was a murder at Indian Lake Park a couple of Saturdays ago?"

"Yeah, some cops interviewed me and my parents. Kids here have been talking about it. Gross."

"I'm interested if you heard or saw anything that Saturday."

"Nothing."

"Were you in the vicinity of the park?"

"Only when I was at home."

"What were you doing that night?"

"Hanging with friends."

"What sort of things do you do when you hang with friends?"

"Drive around, go to somebody's house, watch movies, play video games, play euchre, or sheepshead. We're lucky when we go to Eric's; he's got a pool table."

"Were you at Eric's that Saturday night?"

"No."

"Where'd you go?"

"To Madison. To the mall."

"What did you do there?"

"Walked around. Looked at stores. Ate. The usual."

"Who drove?"

"A couple of us did."

"I've been told your car needs a new muffler."

"Yeah, Dad's promised to fix it after harvest. He said we could still use it until then."

"What time did you get home?"

Ian fidgeted in his chair, looked at Principal Zander, and then down at the floor.

"After my curfew."

"What time is your curfew?"

"Midnight."

"Can you give me a definite time?"

"No, ma'am. I only know that my mother was up and angry when I walked in the door. I was given a few more chores to do last weekend."

"Did you see any cars or people at Indian Lake when you drove home?"

"No, ma'am."

Damn, there was that ma'am again. Thirty was over the hill. Edie handed Ian her business card. "If you remember something, could you or your parents call me at this number?" Edie looked at Principal Zander. "I've got nothing else to ask."

Principal Zander handed a pre-written hall pass to Ian.

Edie waited until Ian left to talk with Principal Zander. "You said he's never been in any trouble."

"None that has been brought to my attention. Ian participates in school activities, but he's not a standout. Nice kid to have around. More of filler-in, a tagalong, than a leader."

"Thanks," said Edie, handing her a business card. "I'll forward a copy of my report on this meeting to you."

Edie left the offices. She was startled by Ian stepping out of the shadows.

"Did you come from talking to my mom?"

"Yes. Why?"

"Next time, change your clothes before coming into the school. Some of the kids don't understand about farming. The barn smells follow you. The other kids made a few jokes. That's why I stopped milking in the morning," said Ian, then hurried to his class.

Edie sat in the school's parking lot, absorbed in writing notes. She shifted her gaze to the left as two teens, in a car that surely had belonged to someone's grandmother, parked next to her. The passenger pulled a wad of money from an inner pocket of his jacket, fanned the wad. Edie was sure that she saw a few one-hundred dollar bills in that stack. Then he peeled off one bill, and handed it to the driver.

Edie continued writing notes until the kids left their car. She counted one Mississippi, two Mississippi, all the up to ten Mississippi, and then lifted her head and watched as the boys entered the school. She waited another five minutes before getting out of her car. She jotted down the license number and car make and model before heading back to school. She hoped that she had given the boys enough time to melt into a classroom.

Edie was buzzed back into school with instructions to go to the office. When there she was informed that she'd have to wait a few minutes. Principal Zander was busy.

Edie reviewed the school menu, the events for the week, looked over the sign–out sheet. She caught the eye of a secretary. "Wanted to ask Principal Zander about Ian Boehnen's friends. I forgot to ask her about his friends."

"Principal Zander wouldn't be the one to ask about friendships between the students. She deals with discipline. Ian's a nice kid, polite, doesn't get into trouble. I think he hangs around with Sean Coyle and with one of the Esser kids."

"And that Theis kid," said the other secretary, pounding her keyboard.

"Which one?" asked the first secretary.

"Eric, LeRoy and Madonna's kid."

"I can't believe that."

"Neither did I, but there they were at the grocery store, together. Wouldn't have believed it, if I hadn't seen it with my own eyes."

"Maybe Ian will be a good influence on Eric."

"Maybe," said the second secretary.

"Can I get Eric's number?" Edie asked.

"Sorry, I don't think we can give that out," said the first secretary.

"That's okay, I'll ask Principal Zander for it," said Edie.

The second secretary walked to the counter, picked up the sign-out sheet, and slid a note toward Edie.

Edie pulled out her notebook, jotted down the names the secretaries had given her, slid the note into her book, looked at her watch. "Sorry to have bothered you ladies, but I have to go. I'll talk to the principal later." Edie quickly left the building.

In the car, Edie looked at the note, Eric's and his parents' numbers. She flipped through her notes on the case. She was right, the Theises hadn't been interviewed.

She punched in Theis's name on her mobile data terminal, now standard equipment in every squad. Edie tried to find something to complain about computers in the squad, the only thing she could find was one more acronym to memorize, MDT. The machine displayed an address for LeRoy and Madonna Theis. Edie decided to pay the Theises a visit.

The Theis place, almost at the top of a hill, looked like a storybook farm. The barn was painted red and white, the lawn immaculate. The house could have been showcased in an architectural or garden magazine. The two-story house was built from local sandstone with a wide inviting porch, a dining room, obviously an addition, designed to capture the valley view, a place to see and be seen. The sweeping brick path invited guests to the front entrance. This was not a working farm, it was picture-perfect.

Edie used the back door. A casually dressed middle-aged woman answered the doorbell.

"Mrs. Theis . . ." said Edie.

"Sorry, I'm not Mrs. Theis. I'm her housekeeper. May I tell her who is calling?"

"Detective Edie Swift with the sheriff's department," said Edie, handing the woman a business card.

Edie was left staring at the outside of the back door. She turned around to look at the farm buildings, and added to her future plans: buy the view from her kitchen and hire a gardener to take care of it.

The door opened and Edie was admitted to the kitchen. A slender blonde woman in winter white slacks and a pale pink sweater stood by the table with her hand extended. Edie quickly shook the soft manicured hand, and felt as if there was an expectation to drop to one knee and kiss the rock that dominated the proffered hand. Edie ignored the silent command.

"I'm Mrs. Theis. Is there something I can do for you?"

"I'm Detective Edie Swift. I'm investigating the murder at Indian Lake Park."

"And we are of interest because . . . ?"

"I've heard that your son, Eric, is friends with a boy who lives near the park."

"Should I be concerned about this?"

"Not at all. You know how teenagers are, give them a car, and they drive all over the country."

"That is true. Eric and his Jeep are inseparable."

"I thought that Eric and his friend might have been cruising near the park and heard or saw something that night that might help me. With this encompassing view of the valley, maybe you or your husband saw something?"

"I'm sorry. I cannot help you there. My husband and I were at a party at the governor's mansion that night; we didn't get home until late. Eric was in bed when we got home."

"Do you remember the time?"

"It was after two a.m."

"May I talk with Eric?"

"No. Eric's in school at the moment, and I doubt my husband will give you permission to talk to him."

"May I talk with Mr. Theis?"

"No, Roy is out playing farmer."

Edie looked confused.

"My husband is out combining."

"Is there a better time to reach him?"

"I will give him your card. He will call you."

Edie was ushered out of the kitchen, and again stood looking at the outside of the kitchen door.

She looked at her watch. Time to pick up Hillary. An interview with Sean Coyle would have to wait.

Aunt Jill was raking leaves into an already huge pile when Edie pulled up in her own car. Edie had a desire to run and jump into it. What the hell. She ran, jumped, sending the leaves flying around the yard.

"Look what you've done to my leaves! Are you going to rake them back up?" Aunt Jill tried to sound angry.

Edie brushed leaves from her hair and clothes as she leaned in to kiss Aunt Jill.

"Don't you come near me smelling like that. Where have you been?" Aunt Jill asked, pushing her away.

Edie lifted her arm to her nose. Ian Boehnen was right. It was hours ago since she had been in the Boehnen farm, and yet the odors lingered.

"And don't go into my house. I'll bring Hillary and all her things out to you."

"But it's about time for her to eat."

"You think she'll eat when you smell like that?"

"If she's hungry enough."

"I guess you can sit on the back porch."

"We'll freeze."

"No, Hillary will be fine. You'll freeze. I'll put the space heater out there and give you some blankets. You are not coming into this house."

Aunt Jill went into the house. Edie dutifully went around to the back and waited for Aunt Jill to unlock the door.

Edie settled into a chair with Hillary while Aunt Jill searched for the heater.

The heater was started. Two blankets covered Edie as she nursed Hillary and Aunt Jill set out a mug of hot chocolate and hot buttered toast for Edie. It was a good day.

"How's your case coming?"

"Not sure yet," said Edie. "Interviewed a few people, that's all."

"Anything falling into place?"

"Nope."

"It will."

The women sat silent on the porch enjoying the company of each other.

Edie broke the silence, "Phil's mother wants us to baptize Hillary."

"Nothing wrong with that. You were."

Edie picked her jaw off the floor. "When did that happen?"

"When you were a baby. Your grandmother kept hounding me until I gave in. It didn't harm you—or me. And it got your grandmother off my back."

"Why didn't we go to church?"

"Wasn't having you baptized enough for getting into the kingdom? It was enough for my mother. Are you going to invite me to the party when it happens?"

"If you promise to watch what you say."

"I can be civil. How about Lorraine?"

"That's Phil's problem. But Phil and I still have to talk about this baptism thing." Edie started to chuckle. "Poor Lorraine, she can't call me a heathen anymore."

Edie smiled down at her nursing daughter. She broke suction and shifted her to the other breast. When done, Edie met Aunt Jill's gaze.

"Your mother doesn't know what she's missing," said Aunt Jill.

"Did she ever?"

"No. From the time I knew her, my sister was full of herself, she never had room for anyone else."

The women dropped the subject. They would pick it up, as they always did, another time.

"Have you decided on a name?" Edie asked.

"I thought you named her Hillary. But if you want me to name her, I will."

"You know what I mean."

"That's really up to you. What do you want your daughter to call me?"

"Granny."

"Sounds old to me."

"It sounds comfortable to me. If you don't like Granny, how about Nana, Grandmom, Grandmother . . ."

"I'm not really her grandmother."

"Yes, you are."

Aunt Jill thought for a moment. "Granny, it is. And to hell with what your grandmother might have said."

"Then Granny it will be," Edie said.

"What will Lorraine say?"

"Who cares? This is between you and me, and we've decided."

18

✳

Hillary was sleeping in the Pack'n Play. The wood stove warmed the back room and supper was in the oven. The only one missing was Phil, who was late coming home from work.

Edie met him at the door with a kiss.

"What was that for?" asked Phil.

"Why isn't a kiss just a kiss?"

"Because I know you. With you, a kiss isn't always just a kiss. But, for the record, you can kiss me anytime. Come here and do it again."

Edie kissed him again. "Supper's ready. I'll put it on the table while you wash up."

Phil did as he was told. At the table, he took the chair nearest the wood stove. The walk home from the shop had been cold. He took a deep breath and plunged in. "Thought you were going to State Street tonight?"

"Change of plans. I'm going tomorrow night." Edie paused, holding the casserole dish in midair. "There is something I'd like you to do for me."

"I knew it. I knew there was something you wanted from me from the moment you kissed me. Kisses never lie. You lied to me."

"What lie did I tell?"

"That you wanted to kiss me."

"That wasn't a lie."

"But there was more to it than just a kiss."

"So I didn't complete the thought. An error of omission," she said, placing the casserole on the table.

"I did enjoy the kiss. Tell me what you want."

"You to come with me . . . to a football game."

"Who's playing?"

"Victor Berger High and some other school."

"Those are at night. Hillary's too young to take to a game. Do you know how far it is? And . . . and . . ." Surprised by the request, Phil searched for other objections.

"And?"

"I don't want to go nor do I need to relive my high school years." Phil should've started with those objections first of all. He kept forgetting that it was best to get down to the nitty–gritty with Edie, fast.

"Everybody else seems to want to, why not you? Come on, you like sports."

"Yes, in the comfort of someone's living room. Why do you want to go?"

"Work. Those kids at Victor Berger High are starting to interest me. I interviewed a kid at the high school today. While I was sitting in the parking lot a teenager in the next car pulled out a wad of money, peeled off a hundred-dollar bill, and handed it to a friend like it was pocket change. Where did he get that much money?"

"Even I could make a good guess where he got that much money. Did you arrest him?"

"On what charge?"

"Possession of more money than a teenager should have. He'll probably just go spend it."

"Not a crime. But it is interesting. I want to see these kids in their natural setting. Please, come. I need you for cover."

"Who's going to watch Hillary?"

Edie knew she and Phil would be going to next Friday's football game.

"Aunt Jill. Eat your dinner, it's getting cold."

19

✳

Edie carefully selected the clothes she was going to wear on the visit to State Street: jeans, still maternity jeans, but no one would know that as a long T-shirt and a longer bulky sweater covered them. And her winter shell would cover those. And wool socks. Christ, she was earning the ma'am that the kids were calling her. Phil called from across the hall.

"Do we have any disposable diapers?"

"Second shelf under the changing table."

"How many diapers does Hillary go through in a night?"

"Depends, two to four."

"Where are her clothes? My sisters always say they take an extra outfit with them."

Edie crossed the hall to investigate.

"What are you doing?"

"With you gone, I'd thought Hillary and I would go visit my mother." Phil kept his head down to avoid Edie's expression.

"That's fine. Why would I object to Hillary visiting her grandmother? Just remember whose kid she is. Ours. And she's there for a visit and nothing else."

"My mother wouldn't do anything without our permission."

"Wanna make a bet?"

Phil declined, he did know his mother. Edie chose two outfits and a sleeper with a sleeping bag for the ride home, some diapers, some butt wipes, and stuffed them into the diaper bag. She went to the kitchen, brought back three packets of breast milk and a cold pack, adding them to the bag. She dropped two pacifiers into a side pouch, and then handed the bag to Phil.

"That should cover you," said Edie.

"All that for one little baby?" said Phil.

"What, you don't think it's enough?" Edie went back to dressing for the night.

Phil quizzed her before she left the house.

"Is your cell charged and on?"

"Yes."

"Do you have your gun?"

"Yes."

Edie kissed them goodnight, flung the backpack over one shoulder and headed into the dark.

Edie sat in her car, waiting for someone to exit the Francis Street parking ramp. She'd forgotten about the home football game. It was a duh moment for Edie. Saturday equals football, where was her head? Five minutes into the wait, one car exited, one car entered, that left two cars in front of her and nowhere for her to turn around—the street was full of cars and partiers. Must have won the game, thought Edie, but this was Madison. We could've lost and everybody was drowning their sorrows. Except for Edie, who sat in her car and fumed.

Edie did get into the ramp, finally, and found the only legal parking space on the top floor. Edie looked over the rooftops of central Madison. Once upon a time, the view was unobstructed from the Capitol, at one end of State Street, to Bascom Hall, Van Hise and Van Vleck at the other end. Now tall buildings dotted her Madison. She shook her head. She didn't want to be one of those Madisonians who never wanted change, but couldn't some part of central Madison stay human–sized?

Coming out of the ramp, Edie looked right, and then left. Bars anchored both ends of the street. She decided to go right, toward University Avenue. After showing her driver's license, she pushed her way to the bar, asked to talk with someone who worked last Saturday. She was pointed to one of the waitresses.

The waitress was busy. Edie stepped in front of her to stop her for a second.

"This will just take a second," said Edie.

"Seconds cost me money. Can you be quicker?"

"Sure." Edie pulled Washington's picture from her coat pocket. "Ever seen this man in here?"

The waitress looked at the photo for a moment, "No," and handed the photo back and walked toward a table waving at her.

"Would you look again? I was wondering if he was in here last Saturday after the game."

"Ma'am, I would remember the guy if he had been a big tipper, had to be thrown out, or was one of my regulars. See this crowd? It's the same every home football game. See that guy at the end of the bar? He's been coming here since before I started. That group over there, the ones holding up the wall, at least one of them will get drunk and the lot of them will get thrown out, they do it every home game. The man in your photo, I don't remember. Sorry. Excuse me, I've gotta get back to work. I'm losing money standing here." The waitress put on a smile, drew her shoulders back, put her hips into action and walked to the table of drunks waving at her.

"Thanks!" Edie shouted after her. Edie left the bar and walked to the bar at the other end of the street.

It was the same story in that bar: students, alumni, and Wisconsin football fans crowded together. The guy in the picture wasn't a regular, not rowdy, not drunk, not thrown out, not memorable, according to a waitress who Edie could get to stand still.

It was, also, the same story in each of the fifteen bars Edie stopped at. No one had seen the man in the photo. There were more bars around the square that she could visit, but it was after ten and she'd come up with zilch so far. And she wanted to go home. She didn't want to pump in one more bathroom. She stood at the top of State Street, still crowded, remembering when this was fun. She sighed, pushed through the crowds as she walked down State to her car.

Edie sat in her car, waiting to get out of the parking ramp. The line to get out was longer than the line had been to get in. The thought occurred to Edie to park the car and try again later. But if she gave up her spot now, who knew when she would get out of the ramp. She stayed in line.

If she hadn't been so tired and closed her eyes for a moment, Edie wouldn't have been surprised by some guy wearing red and white-striped bib overalls tapping on her car window. It took a few seconds for Edie to register that the Badger fan was Fred Price. She thought he only owned white shirts, dark ties, and black suits. She rolled down her window.

"My car's down a few spaces, can you wait and let me in line?" asked Fred.

"Not your day, is it? I've already let two cars in and I'm guessing the people behind me are ready to lynch me."

"I wouldn't let that happen. See anything?"

"Nope, wasn't my day, either."

"I struck out, too. Care to reconsider letting me in line?"

"Not on your life. I've been inching along for twenty minutes now. Suffer like the rest of us." Edie rolled up her window, ignored Fred, and inched her car forward.

Phil beat Edie home by a few seconds. His car was still running when she parked behind him. She got out to help him carry the baby and her stuff into the house.

"How'd your night go?" asked Phil.

"Same as last time, no one saw Russell Washington. How was yours?"

"Good. A couple of my sisters came over with their kids. They all said hi and that Hillary is beautiful. One refused to hold her, said that babies were catching and that she had enough. Mom sent home enough food for the next week."

Edie released the car seat from its base and carried Hillary into the house. Phil followed with the diaper bag and food. Edie ignored the obnoxious phone beeping, indicating a message was waiting, and settled into the glider to nurse Hillary.

Phil hit the message button. "Hi, this is Jerome Adler, I think I've got the right number for Edith Swift. I've got some film you might want to see. Give me a call to arrange the time." He forgot to leave his phone number, but Edie decided to worry about that tomorrow. Tonight she wanted to curl up next to someone warm and sleep.

20

＊

Hillary and Edie were up at six the next morning, Edie wondered if it was too early to call a farmer. She'd learned the hard way that it was too early to call anyone that lived in town; if she was awake at six, why wasn't everyone else? She waited until the more sane hour of nine to call. She got his wife, Mary Adler, who said that Jerome had milked and gone to the fields hours ago. Luckily, Mary Adler knew what Edie was talking about and arranged for her to come during Sunday Night football, anytime.

Edie went alone to the Adlers. Born and raised in the city, where streetlights anchored each corner, Edie was always astounded at the darkness of night and the multitude of stars that were visible away from the city lights. But these days she was grateful for the yard lights of farms that pierced the dark and brought comfort to a single traveler on country roads. Edie pulled into the Adlers' dooryard and parked where the yard light shown brightest.

Edie pounded on the door, waited, and then pounded again. She turned around, no lights were on in the shop or barn. She knew that the house had a front entrance, but it looked as if it was never used. She couldn't see any other entrance. She knocked again. Jerome Adler flipped on the outside light, peeked through the curtain, and then opened the door.

"How long you been standing out here?"

"Not long," Edie lied.

"Come on in." Edie followed him into the house. She could hear the Packer game was still on, second down and four yards to go. Jerome stopped at the fridge. "Can I get you a beer?

"What do you have?"

"Most anything: porter, stout, lager, pilsner, IPA, hefeweizen, ale, and some pumpkin brew" he said, sorting through the beer bottles.

"The ale, thanks."

Jerome handed her a bottle. "If you don't mind, I'll bring the movie up during halftime. I'd like to see the rest of this quarter."

Edie nodded as she followed Jerome into the living room. The TV was huge and blaring. A woman she took to be Mary Adler was sitting on the couch. They smiled at each other. Edie took a seat as far away from the TV as would be polite. There were ten minutes left in the second quarter. If she took a few sips now, watched Adler's video, she'd be well within the legal alcohol limit and could still see most of the second half of the game at home. Edie took a couple of sips, set the bottle on the floor out of sight, and cheered on the Packers.

At halftime Jerome Adler heaved himself out of his chair and turned to Edie. "The computer's in the office. Like another beer before I show you the video?"

"No, thanks, game was exciting, barely touched the first," said Edie.

Adler looked at his wife and shouted, "Coming with us to the office?"

Mary took out her earplugs. "I'm sorry, what did you say?"

"I'm showing this detective the video."

"Lead the way," said Mary, pushing herself out of her chair.

The office was just a few steps away. Edie looked around for a chair, but they were all piled with paper. Jerome dropped a stack of papers on the floor and offered the chair to Edie. Mary looked over Edie's shoulder.

"Just take a few moments to boot. Interesting video. Mary recognized a few of the kids. With our kids grown, I don't know many of the young people these days."

"Here it is. That's me and there's you. That's the day I put the camera up. Got a few nice-sized bucks going past since that day. It's what's near the end that I wanted you to see."

Edie watched as deer, raccoons, and possums nosed around under the camera. Most of the footage was of trees and brush. Adler was right, near the end of the video four people had walked past the camera.

"Would you play that again?"

As the animals nosed around the oak tree on the film, Edie pulled her chair closer to the screen and took control of the computer. Edie froze the video at the frame when the four people entered the camera range.

"Mary, can you identify anyone?"

"One of the kids is Ian Boehnen, he helped us with haying last year. One of the kids carrying a rifle could be a Theis kid. Don't know which one. There are lots of Theises in the area. Don't recognize the other kid carrying a rifle."

"I'd say that one was an Esser kid. Looks like a few of the Essers that I went to school with," said Jerome.

"Now that you say that, I can see the Esser in one kid. The man, I have no idea who that is. There are so many subdivisions going in around here, I don't know the town like I used to," said Mary.

"Could I get a copy of this?" Edie asked.

"Sure. Mary, where do we keep the blank DVDs?"

Mary nudged Jerome and Edie out of the way, opened a desk drawer, pulled out a stack of blank DVDs, popped one in the computer, and burned a copy for Edie. Mary held the DVD out for Edie.

"Do you have a plastic bag to put that in?" Edie asked.

Mary came back with a quart-sized bag, dropped the packaged DVD into it.

Edie wrote a receipt for the DVD received from the Adlers.

"Thanks," said Edie as she wrote date, time, and place on the outside of the bag. "Do you have Internet connection out here?"

"Yes," said Mary. "Not always a good one. Better when the leaves are off the trees. Why?"

"I'd like you to e-mail me a copy of this video. If you'll log into your account, I'll do the rest."

Jerome moved his chair as far back as he could to give Edie and Mary room to work. Edie wrote a note as to why the video was made, why it was being sent, the possible identities of the kids by Mary and Jerome Adler, date, time, and place. She attached the video, hit send, and closed the e-mail.

"We got proof of those kids trespassing, probably also hunting out of season. I'd like to charge them," said Jerome.

"You can do that, but can you wait until I get back to you? I want to show my boss this video, and kick some ideas around with her," replied Edie.

"Her?"

"Yes, sir, her."

"How many women are on the force?"

"An increasing number. And they are good."

"When are you going to get back to me?"

"Well, I'm thinking next week."

"That's okay, don't want any interruptions until combining is finished."

"Where's the camera now?"

"Put it back in the tree."

"If you get anything else, call me." Edie could hear the game analysis. "Sounds like halftime is almost over, time for me to leave."

"You can watch the rest with us," Jerome offered.

"Thanks for the offer; I've got a kid at home who needs my attention." *And my hearing to save, thought Edie.*

"Drive safe. Careful of the deer, it's rutting season, they're all over the roads this time of year. I'd like to save those bucks for me," said Jerome as he walked her back to the door.

Edie could hear the deadbolt click as she stood on the back step and wondered how long the Adlers had been locking their door. These people needed to know why this murder happened and who did it, fast. They needed to get on with their lives without looking over their shoulders in fear every moment. And yet Edie felt as if she were floating on air as she walked back to her car; maybe this video was the start of finding that peace for these people.

Edie drove home carefully, not because of Adler's warning but because of that video. Scenarios kept popping in her brain, some she rejected, some she tucked away for further consideration. Luckily, she didn't have to worry about traffic—no one else was on the road. Wisconsinites were glued to their TVs, cheering their Pack to another win.

21

*

Packing the diaper bag had almost become automatic, loading the car with baby stuff was becoming routine, and maybe, the thought kept breaking into her thoughts, she should just stay at work instead of finishing her maternity leave. Maybe, instead of an extended maternity leave, Gracie could give her extra days off in the coming year. Sounds like a good plan to me, Edie thought, as she secured the car seat for the drive to Aunt Jill's.

After she left, Edie slapped her forehead. She should have called Fred Price. She put the car into park at the stop sign, rifled through the pump bag, through her pockets, reached back for the diaper bag, and briefly considered checking Hillary's diaper for her cell. She must have left it at home. Okay, maybe she wasn't quite as organized as she thought. Edie drove on. She wouldn't need the phone, and she'd be at the office all day.

At the office, Edie found that Gracie Davis was in a meeting. Fred was busy until about ten thirty. He'd look at what she had then. That left two or so hours for Edie to fill. Most of that time was spent reviewing the video and writing out the possibilities it presented. Edie found that making the scenarios concrete made it easier to decide if they were crazy or not.

After pumping, Edie went looking for Luke Fitzgerald, one of the deputies who patrolled the Indian Lake area. Her luck was changing, he was in.

"How's it going, Luke?" asked Edie.

"Drugs, joyrides, a few car–farm implement accidents."

"Really! Why?"

"Mostly inattentive driving, city folks out for a cruise and not knowing how to share the roads with farm vehicles. Happens every season."

"Anything happening at Victor Berger High School?"

"A few weeks ago the principal had us out to check for drugs. Didn't find anything."

"Only the dumb kids keep the stuff in their lockers."

"I'm kinda busy, you looking for something in particular?"

"Just getting a feel for the territory. An area farmer found a couple of dead deer on his land, wanted to know who was shooting them. He put up one of those game cameras, got some great photos of a few bucks and some kids trespassing. Thought you might know of something brewing in your area."

"Nothing big. Can I take a look at that video?"

"Sure, maybe you can identify the kids."

Luke followed Edie back to her desk. He was real interested in the bucks.

"Look at those antlers. I'd like to hunt that land. Which farmer did you say gave you the video?"

"I didn't. For now this is under wraps. It goes no further than you. Understand?"

"Part of your investigation?"

"Maybe, I'll know soon enough. Here, this is the part I wanted you to look at."

Once again, the three teens and man crossed Edie's monitor.

"Recognize any of them?"

"Play it again, I was thinking about those bucks," said Luke as he moved Edie to one side and plopped his face closer to the monitor. He replayed the video three more times. "One of those kids is Eric Theis. The others I don't know."

"How do you know Eric Theis?"

"Mostly he's trying to make himself the big man on campus—mostly speeding, underage drinking, anything that will make him look like a rebel to impress other kids. He usually settles down for a while after we talk to him. Hope he grows out of that stuff soon, he has the potential be a good kid. Want me to keep an eye on him?"

"That and more. I want you to keep your ear to the ground. Anything out of the ordinary happens, call me."

Edie was waiting in Gracie's office when the lieutenant entered.

"What are you doing in here?" Gracie asked.

"Waiting for you and Fred."

"You know the rule. This is my office, you only come in when I'm here."

"Yes, ma'am."

"What've you found?" she asked, shooing Edie out of her chair and getting comfortable in her ergonomic chair.

"A video taken by a local farmer."

"I hope this is going to crack the case, because the higher-ups are about ready to chew my butt. They want this solved NOW."

"I believe I was invited to this gathering," said Fred Price, as he walked in and took off his coat. "What do you have?"

"I forwarded a video to Lieutenant Davis and myself. It was taken by Jerome Adler. He farms in the Indian Lake area. Part of his farm is on the backside of the park. Adler put up a game camera to catch poachers. I think he caught something more. Was wondering what you two thought of the video."

Gracie opened her e-mail and played the video.

"Looks like some kids trespassing," she said.

"That is what they are doing. Mr. Adler would like to charge them with trespassing when we identify them. Says he'll hold off pressing charges until he hears from me," said Edie.

"You think this is linked to Washington?" asked Fred.

"Could be. Luke Fitzgerald, who patrols that area, ID'd one of the kids as Eric Theis, a troublemaker, but nothing serious—yet. One of the kids is Ian Boehnen, I interviewed him regarding the Washington case. He states that he neither saw nor heard anything that night. The other kid, no positive ID. The older man no one knows, but he is bugging me. Can't put my finger on why," said Edie.

They played the video again.

"Forward that to me, I'll check our databases, but if we don't have anything, it's probably just some people trespassing," said Fred.

"I agree with Fred. This isn't anything. But if you need to check it out, do so. If they aren't doing more than trespassing, maybe they heard or saw something that could help us. Download stills of the boys and that man, pass them around the drug and gang task forces, maybe they know something," Gracie directed. "If nothing comes up, hand this over to the deputy patrolling the area. We can, at least, follow up with that trespassing charge."

"Buy you a cup of coffee?" Fred offered as they left Gracie's office. "I'd like to hear about the interviews you did."

"Where do you want to talk?"

"Break room."

"Then I'll just have water, I drink that coffee as a last resort."

Fred bought coffee for himself and a bottle of water for Edie. Both sat with their backs to the wall so that the entire room was visible. They wanted to know who came in and who lingered in hopes of catching some information.

"Tell me about Ian Boehnen," said Fred.

"Farm kid, from what his mother and the Adlers say, he works hard. Haven't interviewed Mr. Boehnen yet, hope to set one up this week. Victor Berger High School principal states that Ian Boehnen's never been in trouble at the school. The high school secretaries agree with that, but they don't like Eric Theis, a friend of Ian's—I get the impression they consider him trouble."

"You said you interviewed Ian Boehnen."

"Yes, at Victor Berger High School with the principal in attendance. I think he lied at one point, said he couldn't remember what time he got home the night of the murder, just that it was past his curfew."

"What do you make of it?"

"Not a thing. It's just an interesting observation . . . for now."

Fred dumped his half–full cup of coffee, and then stopped at the door. "This case hasn't opened up at all. Maybe these photos will help. I'll get back to you about them. Give me a call after you talked to Ian's father."

"Sure thing," said Edie. Maybe Gracie and Fred didn't think anything of the video, but she did. Her gut was telling her that this case was opening up.

Edie followed Gracie's suggestions. She downloaded a number of still photos of the four trespassers and took it over to the drug task force.

She found one member, Jeff, at his desk, typing out a report with the hunt–and–peck method. Jeff stopped typing after Edie cleared her throat for the second time.

"Thanks for the break from this damned report. These damned computers aren't any better than a typewriter . . . except when I have to correct mistakes." Jeff paused for a moment. "If I'd known how much paper-work this job involved, I might not have joined the force. What do you need?"

Edie showed him the photos. "Recognize any of these guys?"

"No, none of these guys are on my radar. Should they be?"

"Don't know. I'm just trying to shake something loose."

"Think they're involved in the Washington case?"

"Why would you ask that?"

"Everyone knows that's your only case."

"No clue if they are involved. But I did see something interesting out at Victor Berger High School last week. While I was waiting in my car, saw a young man pull a wad of bills from his jacket, more than someone his age should have."

"See any transactions taking place?"

"Only thing that happened was this teen peeled off a hundred-dollar bill and handed it to the other teen in the car."

"Did the money kid get anything in return?"

"Not that I saw."

"Interesting. Not a good sign, but not illegal. Could be drug money. Some of these teenagers make more money in that trade than their parents do at an old-fashioned job. Want me to check it out for you?"

"Yes, thanks," said Edie, writing out the license number and make and model of the vehicle.

"Got a year on the car?"

"Never acquired that knowledge."

"You and my wife. I'll see what comes up." He went back to pecking out his report.

Edie didn't have any luck with the gang task force, they were all out. She left a note and hoped that they would get back to her sooner than later. She then went in search of Ben Harris.

Ben didn't see Edie come into the department, he was talking to Sadie. But Sadie saw her and continued to ask Ben questions. Ten more questions to be exact. Edie counted them. And each question was the same, asked slightly different, but still the same. Did Sadie think she was being profound? After the tenth question and before Sadie could formulate an eleventh, Edie cleared her throat and tapped Ben on the shoulder.

"Excuse me, I hope I'm not interrupting something," said Edie.

"No, we are just finishing," said Ben.

When Sadie was safely at her desk, out of range of their conversation, Ben whispered to Edie, "Thanks." He continued at a louder pitch. "What can I do for you, Edie?"

"Can you print some quality photos for me?"

"Yes, how many do you need?"

"Give me a handful of each."

"Where are these photos?"

Edie handed the disk over to Ben.

"Interesting package. Is this evidence in your case?"

"Could be."

"So, I need to include this in Washington's file?"

"I think it belongs there. I'll also e-mail you the file version of that, it was sent to me by the Adlers."

"Finally getting a break?"

"Maybe."

"I love that you're not assuming anything."

"You know the saying: if you assume, you make an ass out of you and me."

"You want to wait here or should I bring the photos to your desk?"

Edie eyed Sadie. "Bring them over."

There was a phone message waiting for Edie at her desk. Mr. Boehnen would be combining near the home farm tomorrow, if Edie still wanted to interview him. Edie called Patricia Boehnen back. It was settled, the interview would be tomorrow morning at nine thirty. Edie was to stop by the house and get directions to the field. Also, wear clothes she didn't mind getting dirty.

Edie spread the photos Ben dropped off across her desk. She stared at each, memorizing each face, letting her mind linger over each scenario that popped into her head. Each scenario possible, but nothing concrete, except for these photos. Edie knew that she had to retrace her steps, again.

With Hillary in the co-sleeper and the baby monitor on, Edie assessed her house—messy. How could one little baby disrupt the schedules of two adults? Should she pick up now or wait until Hillary was in college, as Aunt Jill suggested? Eighteen years was a long time to wade through stacks of newspapers, catalogs, toys, coffee cups, and whatever else that had been shoved under the furniture. Edie cleaned the house, somebody had to, but it was for the last time, she thought. The next cleaning was someone else's problem. The next somebody was Phil.

When Phil came home from work, he was ordered to halt, not to come into the house wearing his filthy work boots, and to drop his clothes in the laundry. Edie didn't care if he had to streak naked through the house. Phil dropped his clothes in the laundry and headed for the bedroom, but didn't make it. He was stopped by the aromas of supper, it smelled like stew and pumpkin something—he hoped it was pumpkin pie. Phil strolled butt-naked through the rest of the house to the kitchen to investigate the enticing aromas.

"You're late," said Edie.

"I left a message." Phil saw a slight blush creep across Edie's face. "Didn't take the phone with, did you?"

"No. I can handle life without a cell."

"I can't. Take yours with you," Phil, still naked, stood and argued with Edie.

Naked bodies didn't bother Edie, especially not his, but she reminded him of their neighbor's habit. "We may not have many cars going past our house to stare at your butt, so I'm wondering whose eye candy you want to be? Mine or Mrs. Voss'?"

Phil hotfooted it to the bathroom.

Clean and dressed, Phil returned to the kitchen, where Edie was setting the table. "We having company?"

"No."

"Why the clean house and this delicious–smelling food?"

"Because this is the way WE are going to keep it."

"But I'm tired when I get home."

"So am I."

"I don't know how to cook."

"Do you know how to read?"

"Yes." Phil saw where this was going, but he couldn't stop it—he wasn't Superman.

"Have you ever taken a chemistry class?"

"Yes."

"Then you can cook. Learn. I'll give you an early Christmas present to help."

"What if I don't want to?"

Edie stopped stirring the stew. "There's always a reason to return to your mother."

"What if I don't want to do that either?"

"Them's the choices, take 'em or leave 'em."

Phil didn't like the choices. He preferred snuggling up to Edie than sleeping in the back bedroom at his mother's house and being fussed over by her as if he were a little boy. The new world order that was being presented to him was unappealing—step up to being an adult forever and always. Damn.

"How'd your day go?" Phil asked.

"Good. Not great, but good. I'd almost forgotten how much I like this job. Been thinking about going back to work full time now."

"What about your pinkie swear?"

"I remember that silly thing."

"You gave your word."

"And I'll honor it. This is just notice that things change, now. The baby is ours, the house is ours, and the responsibility for both is ours."

Phil sat at the table for supper. He'd experienced how forceful Edie was when she first slapped handcuffs on him during an arrest, their now infamous beginning, just as he learned her softness in the years that followed. Phil had some thinking to do. Damn, one more giant step into adulthood.

22

*

It was 9:15 a.m. when Edie arrived at the Boehnen's home. Time, she figured, to make things go her way. Time to make things fit into her schedule. She walked to the barn, no one would be in the house, someone was probably still doing chores. She was right. Patricia Boehnen was finishing chores. Edie was directed up the road, first field road to the left, take the field road about half a mile back. Karl was expecting her.

The field road was bumpy, Edie thought it would be easier to get out and walk but didn't see a place she could pull off and park the car. She hoped Hillary would appreciate the milkshake that was being made just for her.

The combine was at the far end of the field when Edie finally parked her car. Not far from the combine a tractor and a huge wagon were parked. She walked over there to wait. Edie was intrigued as she watched the cornstalks pulled into the machine and kernels of corn dropped into the bin and the chewed-up cornstalks spewed out the back of the machine. Edie thought Mr. Boehnen would stop at the end of the row. He didn't. He turned the machine and went back down the field. It wasn't until the combine bin was full that he drove over to the cart, swung an auger over the cart, and emptied the combine of corn. Mr. Boehnen opened the cab door, swung the ladder out, and motioned for Edie to join him.

"I'm Karl Boehnen. Patricia said to watch for you," he said. He waited for Edie to settle into the buddy seat, and then reached across her to slam the combine door shut. "Sorry about not stopping, but I'd like to finish this field while it's light. Patricia says you want to talk to me." He finished unloading the corn, swung the auger in, and maneuvered the combine back to the standing corn.

"I've read what you told the other deputy, just want to go over it again."

"Sure, but don't mind me if I have to get out to adjust stuff."

"Fine with me. Have you heard about what happened at Indian Lake?"

"Yes. That's replaced talk about the weather and grain prices at the elevator. Everyone's speculating who done it."

"Heard anything interesting?"

"No, just that a black man was killed. Most think it was some gang stuff from Chicago."

"Interesting. I've got a few questions about the Saturday Mr. Washington was killed. Did you see or hear anything over in the park?"

"Like I said before, I didn't hear or see anything over in the park or on my road that night."

"How late were you working?"

"I was in bed by ten, don't like to be on the road at night on the weekends."

"Why not?"

"More drunks than usual are on the road then. And too many of those damn drivers think these roads were made for them—these roads were made for us farmers to get our stuff to market. Also, they don't respect the rules of the road. And they don't respect farmers. Last year some jerk rear-ended my combine. I had my flashers on, the slow-moving vehicle sign was in plain sight, and he still rear-ended the combine. Shut me down for a while until I could find one to rent while mine was being repaired. Damn city folks."

"Sounds like an occupational hazard."

"Shouldn't be. Drivers should get their heads out of their asses when they're in farm country."

Edie chose to ignore his rant and get on with her questions. "Does your son Ian help out on the farm?"

"During the week he works with Patricia. With daylight hours getting shorter, she doesn't like him to be on the road with these damn idiots."

"Does he help on the weekends?"

"Always. He's a good kid."

"Have you met any of his friends?"

"Sean and Ted, haven't had time to meet the others."

"What are Sean and Ted's last names?"

"Sean Coyle and Ted Esser, both farm boys."

"Why not the other boys?"

"I farm and Ian tells me that his other friends don't want to come to the farm, they don't like the smells of a dairy farm."

"Do you know what time Ian got home that Saturday night?"

"Patricia tells me that it was late, so I got him up early and had him work with us all day. We can't afford to sleep till noon around here. Better that Ian learns that now."

Edie thought about that for a while, farms always looked serene, tucked in the country. She was learning there was more to farming than the scenery.

"You're asking a lot of questions about Ian."

"From what you and your wife say, he was the only one off the farm that night. He might have heard or seen something that might help us."

"That might be. Patricia says that he's picking up a social life, out with his friends most Friday nights. She says it's good for him. She says a kid needs to get off the farm once in a while."

"Do you know where he goes on Friday nights?"

"High school games, hanging with friends, I guess."

"What did you do at that age?"

"Worked. Did get out to a few games, and family stuff, but mainly worked. Didn't hurt me none."

But you probably didn't have much fun either, thought Edie. Time to change the subject. "Nice combine, my first time in one."

"It's taken me a long time to get one like this. Wished I had that buddy seat you're on for Ian when he was little, he might've enjoyed riding with me. Now, I don't bother to ask him."

"Kids do grow up."

"Faster than I knew," said Karl Boehnen, as he swung the combine and auger to unload the bin of corn into the cart. "Want to go another round or two?"

"Thanks, it was interesting, but I need to get back to the office." Edie climbed down and watched as Karl Boehnen went back to combining. She wondered why anyone chose that life, but then people often wondered the same thing about her job.

The interview with Karl Boehnen played over and over and over in Edie's mind, all the way to Madison. It was obvious that Karl Boehnen was a hard worker, that he enjoyed his work, enjoyed his family. Edie was beginning to understand how entrenched the *Kinder, küche, kirche* philosophy was in Karl Boehnen and Phil's world. But how did this play out for Ian? Was Ian caught in a cultural sea change? Did it really have anything to do with her investigation? The interview with Karl wasn't falling in place for Edie. As she adjusted the seat's armrest, Edie caught a whiff of the barn. "Damn, I'd only been in the barn a few minutes and the odor's still clinging to my clothes. Double damn, Aunt Jill will never let her in the house." Poor Ian, thought Edie, searching for her cell to call Aunt Jill and give her a heads–up. She found it in the breast pocket where Phil had jammed it that morning. She got the point; he wanted to stay in touch. No, that wasn't it, as he hadn't called or texted her that morning. He wanted to know that he could stay in touch.

23

*

Edie decided to stay home Wednesday morning. She had spent the weekend working the field. In fact, she had worked the last few weekends out in the field. She wondered if she was getting overtime for those weekend hours or if it was part of the deal she had struck with Lieutenant Gracie Davis. But there were things to be done. The first item on her list was a call to Fred, giving a report on her interview with Karl Boehnen. He reported that nothing popped up on his databases about any of the people from the video. Once they got a name for the man from the video, he'd run that through the files.

There were no messages from the gangs task force on her work cell. There was nothing to do until someone called her. With her conscience quieted, Edie spent her day playing with Hillary and catching up with her reading. By the time Phil got home, Edie had cabin fever. Phil did a juggling act to keep Hillary from hitting the floor as Edie, in jogging clothes, sped past him when he opened the door. Spending all day in the house, Edie needed a run, desperately.

Edie headed toward Troutbeck. She jogged in place at the corner with the empty store, there was a steady line of cars creeping through Troutbeck driven by teenagers. They must know that this is a speed trap, thought Edie. During a break in the traffic, Edie sprinted to the other side of the road and continued her jog in the village.

Edie ran through the section of Troutbeck which was huddled near the church, twice, and then realized what she really wanted was a talk with Carole. Edie ran in place while waiting for Carole to answer the knock on her door.

"Come on in, it's cold out there," Carole said. "I was in the kitchen making supper. Come on back so I can finish getting it in the oven."

Edie followed her and stood next to the stove for more warmth.

"You look cold. Why do wear such skimpy stuff?"

"This running gear is plenty warm, while I'm running."

"Then why are you hugging my stove?"

"I've stopped running. The stove is now warmer than me."

Carole could only shake her head in disbelief. "Can I get you something else to help warm you up?"

"No thanks. How about a trim?"

"It doesn't look like you need one," Carole said eyeing Edie's hair.

"Then can you just wash it?"

"I've got some time. Let's go on into the back."

Edie settled into one of the wash chairs while Carole turned on the water.

"What are all those cars in the village for?" Edie asked, as Carole started the water.

"The Halloween house."

"What?"

"I thought you knew about the Halloween house. It belongs to the high school principal. Every year the kids drive past it, lots of them. They call it the witch's house. I wish somebody would do something about the traffic, we feel like prisoners in our homes around this time of year. Maybe you could?"

"Only if they are breaking the law. More to the point, does anyone leave the village once they're home?" Edie said.

"That isn't the point. We sit a long time at the stop sign for a break in the traffic, until some kid is polite enough to let us through."

"Why not talk with the principal about this?"

"What? That would cause trouble in this quiet little burg."

Edie would never get it, what was the harm in talking?

Carole lowered the chair and ran and massaged warm water through Edie's hair. Edie relaxed.

"Carole, how did you manage to run a business and raise kids?"

"I work where I live. I kept my kids corralled by putting gates throughout the house. I knew where my kids were at all times. I didn't schedule anything during the day that couldn't be interrupted. And when they were sick, got my mother to come help."

"Did Ray help?"

"Yes, but after we had come to the understanding that I wasn't his mother. And the kids were both our responsibility."

"I had that come to Jesus talk last night with Phil."

"You may have to do it a few more times before it sticks."

Edie closed her eyes as Carole massaged her scalp.

"How's the case going?"

"I think I've got a lead. No one else does. It means I'll have to retrace some of my work."

The warm water running through her hair was marvelous. Edie wanted it to last forever. But Carole lifted the chair back to its upright position and combed Edie's hair.

"Anything else you gotta get off your chest?"

"I think I'm going back to work."

"Great. You've made a decision."

"But I feel so torn."

"We all do, well . . . most of us do."

"How do you get past the guilt?"

"You don't. First you get good sitters, and then, when your kids are teenagers, you pass the guilt on to them."

"That's great mothering advice."

"From a great mother," said Carole as she started to blow–dry Edie's hair.

A message from Steve on the Gangs Squad was waiting for Edie when she got home. He'd be working in the office tomorrow morning, nothing that couldn't be interrupted. It went to the top of Edie's to-do list for the next day, she didn't want to miss Steve.

24

*

Hillary went to Aunt Jill's and Edie went to the office.

Steve, from the Gangs Squad, was typing as Edie pulled up a chair and spread the photos on his desk.

"Give me a sec, gotta finish this speech. You know I didn't like making speeches when I was in high school and don't like making them now, but it's become part of the job. Should'a paid more attention to that English teacher back in high school," he said.

Edie was quiet as she watched him type. She had a lot of respect for him. He was good at his job, denying gangs new members by counseling the wandering kids who had been jettisoned by their families, exploring alternatives for kids who found themselves in too deep with gangs. He was a rock for kids who didn't know they were searching for one.

"Congratulations on that new baby. How old is she?"

"Almost eight weeks."

"When you going to bring her in?"

"She's been here a few times already. Why don't you stop by the house to see her?"

"We'll arrange a time later. What do you got for me?"

"These four photos. Does anyone look familiar?"

Steve studied each photo carefully. "No. Tell me about them."

"These were taken from a game camera set up by a farmer. He'd found some dead deer on his property that had been shot and left to rot."

"Not a good sign, but you already know that. Are you thinking your case might be gang–related?"

"Not thinking anything, exploring everything that comes my way, which isn't much, by the way. There's a video I want you to watch. It may be nothing but some guys trespassing. What this video does is gives me two opposing viewpoints of one boy. I don't know if it's any more than that."

"Sometimes I think that all teenagers are bipolar, on top of the world, great fun to be around, next time you see them they're the biggest downers to be around. I'm told it's hormonal."

"Thanks. I'll keep that in the back of my mind for when my baby is that age."

"So, back to the video. What do you know about the boys?"

"Two definitely attend Victor Berger High School. This one is Ian Boehnen." Edie pointed to each picture as she identified the boys. "He's a farm kid. This one's Eric Theis, the secretaries at the school don't like him. According to Luke Fitzgerald, he's starting to get a name. Nothing serious-yet. The third boy, I haven't identified. The man, nothing on him either."

"Have you talked to them?

"Yes, to Ian Boehnen. He's nothing special, a farm kid. Eric's parents won't let me near him. There's money in that family. And political connections."

"Wish you'd seen me first. I could've given you tips on how to approach the boy and his family."

"Left a message for you. Couldn't wait for an answer, needed to move this case forward."

"Do you have the video?"

"Yes, I had it e-mailed to me." Edie brought up the video on Steve's computer.

Steve played it a few times. "Nice bucks. Think the farmer might let me hunt on his land?"

"Not a chance. He wants first crack at them. He's hoping the boys in the video don't get those deer first. So, what do you think about the video?"

"There is always a possibility of gangs out there, hasn't been any active recruitment that I've heard of recently in that area."

"Are these wannabe gang members?"

"In high school, they are no longer wannabes, they are gang members. Let's see what I can surmise from your video. Can't see the clothing color, but it looks as if each boy is wearing something different—a good sign. Gang members tend to wear something similar that can be quickly identified. Don't like that these kids are out late at night. If these are the boys killing those deer, they know it's wrong. They've probably been hunting with their daddies since they were out of diapers. Don't like that an older man is with them. He could be recruiting the boys for a gang, or an older, stupider relative not wanting to move into adulthood." Steve stopped to take a deep breath and sighed. "Looks like the Gangs Squad will be doing more intensive work at that school and community. Who's the principal out there?"

"Zander. Think it's too late for these kids?"

"I hate to give up on teenagers, but we're finding that we have to talk to kids when they are nine and ten years old about gangs, inoculate them early. *Nine- and ten*-year-olds! Kids that age should be worried about baseball, soccer, spelling, and math tests. And we have to talk to them about gangs! Wish we could require parents to attend these talks."

"What do you think my next move should be?"

"Find out more about the kids, keep the Gang Squad informed. We'll talk with the schools, churches, and whatever youth programs are active out there, set up some informational meetings for parents. Wish parents would be more involved with their kids during high school. I'm finding that too many parents drop their kids at the high school doors and wash their hands of their kids until graduation. Those people haven't got the message that parenting is for life. Wish they'd think of that before they make those sweet babies."

"That's not what most people are thinking about at that time," said Edie.

"What are they thinking of?"

"They got an itch that needs to be scratched," said Edie. "Keep me posted on what you're doing, okay?"

"Yes, what are you going to do?"

"Keep digging."

"Be careful, teens are on a hormonal roller coaster." Steve hesitated a moment. "Do you have time to listen to my speech?"

"Sure."

"Don't have much, but here it is: 'When we were teenagers, we were in limbo, in a place between childhood and adulthood. We grouped together as we went in search of adulthood. We followed those who didn't show cowardice, the ones who seemed confident as they negotiated the move out of childhood. We planted cherry bombs, we car surfed, called in bomb scares, and things we still don't whisper about around campfires. Some of us stayed in limbo, some in childhood, some of us made it to adulthood. Some never made it. Your children are now where we were. And their world is a different place.' What do you think? It's supposed to be a five-minute speech."

"I like the KISS principle–Keep It Simple, Stupid. You made your points. Anything more, you'll lose your audience."

"Think so?"

"Yes, don't sugarcoat it."

25

✳

Aunt Jill had agreed to leave her Madison home to babysit Hillary in Troutbeck—the middle of nowhere, and in her mind it was filled with rednecks and worse things that might inhabit that sinkhole. Edie reminded Aunt Jill that she didn't live in the outback, but to be careful driving through Troutbeck. It was known for being a speed trap.

Friday night came, and Edie kept vigil at the picture window for Aunt Jill. There was a sigh of relief when Aunt Jill pulled into the driveway.

Edie showed Aunt Jill where she kept Hillary's stuff, and pointed out the lists: one of emergency phone numbers that might be needed that was taped to the fridge, another list of Hillary's nighttime routine, also taped to the fridge. Only then did Edie exchange car keys with Aunt Jill. And, the most important reminder of all, Edie reminded Aunt Jill that Hillary was to sleep on her back, not some old wife's tale about sleeping on her stomach. These days, back was best.

"Hillary has done fine at my house. Though it's been about thirty years since I took care of a baby, the basics don't change. And I was never an old wife."

"But we'll be on the far side of the county."

"I've got a phone. Do you have yours?"

"I've got mine," Phil piped in. "I'll make sure Edie has hers."

"Now . . . when are you two going to be back?"

"After the game. Can't give you a definite time 'cause I don't remember when they're usually over."

"You don't have to wait for the finish, do you? I'd like to get back to Madison tonight."

"Thought you'd spend the night here."

"I'm prepared to make that sacrifice. You know that I'd do anything for you, but I'd prefer going back to Madison. I'm not used to being in the outback, you can never tell about these inbred rednecks."

Edie kissed Aunt Jill and Hillary and pushed Phil out the door before he burst with laughter.

"I'm not sure it's a good idea for Aunt Jill and my mother to meet," Phil said, sliding into the passenger seat.

"I agree," said Jill backing out of the driveway. "Buckle your seatbelt. But that meeting will happen, hopefully not for another year. Maybe the two of them can focus on Hillary instead of their differences."

"Not sure I want to be there. I'll either die from laughing or get hit by the stuff they'll be throwing at each other."

The Victor Berger High School parking lot was full. Kids were tossing footballs behind the bleachers, others were playing tag. Teens formed circles at a safe distance away from their parents and the younger kids. Parents were greeting each other or getting snacks before the game started. The marching band was warming up. The cheer-leaders were bouncing through their cheers. Edie nodded at Principal Zander as she moved between the groups.

"Different school, but nothing's changed in fourteen years," said Phil as he and Edie looked for a seat at the edge of the bleachers.

"This is how you spent your Friday nights? Did you play?"

"No. And I wasn't in band either. I was one of the geeks standing around in circles trying to look cool. I went to games to be with friends and pick up girls."

Edie looked at the circles of teenagers. "Some things never change."

"Isn't that what it's all about at that age? Picking someone to share the moment with you until you find the someone to share your life."

"Wow, deep thoughts under Friday night lights. What triggered this?"

"High schoolers. They think deep thoughts. Must be catching."

"And I thought we were only dipping ourselves in the hormonal cesspool, not wallowing in it."

"That, too. Which side should we sit on?"

"Find any place near an exit."

The place was packed; Phil thought the game was either a standing rivalry between the schools or home-coming. So Edie and Phil settled for end seats that weren't quite what Edie was looking for, too far up the bleachers for Edie to casually or quickly leave.

Phil watched the game while Edie scanned the side-lines and occasionally left the bleachers to walk among the groups gathered near the edge of the playing field. She watched as a few kids split off from their groups and innocently wandered over to an unused building. She wanted to shout at them that they weren't fooling anybody; everyone knew what those teens were doing, except, hopefully, the young kids who were playing tag. Edie kept quiet. Tonight those kids weren't her business. She bought two hot chocolates and returned to snuggle next to Phil.

"My butt's cold," said Edie, handing Phil his hot chocolate. "I'd tell you to get the blankets from the car, but I forget to put them in Aunt Jill's car."

"That's okay, there are other ways of keeping warm," said Phil as he pulled her closer. "Want to leave?"

"Not yet. Maybe soon, if I don't see any of the kids I'm looking for."

Phil watched the marching band perform. Edie continued to scan the area.

It was when the marching band yielded to the football teams that Edie saw him.

"That's Ian standing behind the end zone. Packer jacket," Edie whispered to Phil.

"Which kid is he? They're all wearing Packer jackets."

"Okay, he's also wearing a red and white hat, standing alone. Now he's walking to his left."

"Okay, I see him now. He's young."

"They all are. Keep an eye on him. I want to see if his parents are in the crowd."

"Won't find them," said Phil.

"Why not?" Edie asked, still scanning the bleachers for Patricia and Karl Boehnen.

"He's a farm kid. Both his parents are working; fall's one of their busiest seasons."

"Damn," said Edie, louder than she meant to. "Why aren't those parents here?"

"Because farm families don't have the luxury of handing their job off to the next shift. If they don't do the job, it doesn't get done. It's a luxury just to let their kids come to the games. In my—"

"Damn, where is he now? Do you see him?"

"Walking over to the concession stand with someone."

"Wonder who he's with," said Edie, pushing her cup into Phil's hand. She dropped to the ground from her place in the bleachers; it was faster than asking the people below them to move to one side. The throngs of kids playing football slowed her movement, but she was able to spot Ian and the older guy as they passed the concession stand. Turn around, she silently pleaded, turn around. Someone shouted to Ian. Ian and the unknown man turned to wait for the boy to join them. Edie stood and watched the three walk into the parking lot. Moments later she heard a car leave the lot. It needed a muffler.

Edie hadn't gotten close enough to hear anything, but she had seen him. Damn it, he was the older man in the video. And she knew she had seen him before, but couldn't place where—yet.

Edie bumped into Principal Zander on her way back to Phil.

"What brings you here?" Principal Zander quizzed Edie.

"Football."

"Anything to do with your case?"

"No, just football," Edie lied. It was the first time in years that she had lied to a school official.

"Would you tell me if it was?"

"No." Edie wanted to stop this line of questioning. "Do you know what that building is used for?" she asked, pointing to where she had seen teen couples casually wander to.

"That's known among the students as the rendez-vous place. Why? Did you see someone going in there?"

"About five minutes ago."

"Damn! The town said they would make sure that building was locked on game nights."

"Guess someone found a way in."

"Double damn, now I've got to go investigate. We don't need any more pregnancies among our students. I'll talk to you later," said Zander and she headed toward the rendezvous building.

Not today, thought Edie, as she went back to the game and Phil. "Let's go, I'm done here."

"Wait a moment; I want to see how they make this play. Fourth down and goal for the home team. Are they going to punt, short pass, quarterback sneak? What?"

Edie looked at the field. "Quarterback sneak."

The ball was snapped. The quarterback stepped back into the pocket. He looked right, and then left. Both of his favorite receivers were open, the frontline did its job blocking. The quarterback cocked his arm as if to throw, and then tucked the ball next to him, wrapped his other arm around it, and then the quarterback scrambled for the daylight that his frontline had created for him. The fake worked. Touchdown for Victor Berger High School.

Following Edie, Phil dropped from the bleachers. "How'd you know that?"

"Obvious. These young quarterbacks can't resist that move. With that one play, the quarterback gets all the glory. The other team should have been prepared for it."

Phil was impressed. "You know about football? You're smart, pretty, tough—what else have you been hiding from me?"

They sat in the running car waiting for their bodies to thaw.

"I've seen that older guy before," said Edie. "Just can't remember where."

"It'll come to you, when your brain thaws."

"If we ever do this again, we drive the car with the butt warmers."

"I can feel my toes now. Do you want to pump while we wait for the rest of me to get warm?" Phil asked.

"My breasts would shrivel if I put anything that cold next to them."

"I don't want that," said Phil, smiling at the teens walking past their car. "Nor do I want these pimply faced boys ogling them."

"Me neither. Let's get out of here; I'm getting depressed about Hillary's teen years."

"We'll start looking for that convent with ten-foot high walls my father threatened my sisters with," said Phil as he eased the car past the knots of teenagers. "What's your next move?'

"Back to State Street tomorrow night."

"Any chance that I can get help with Hillary?"

"I'll call Gracie. She's wanted to come see the house and get her hands on the baby for more than a few moments," said Edie. "State Street!" she yelled. "That's where I saw him, State Street."

26

*

Gracie Davis was more than willing to sit with that sweet baby, as long as she didn't have to eat Phil's cooking. She'd do anything to move this case forward—fast.

At six p.m. sharp, Gracie Davis stepped out of her BMW in uniform and straightened herself to her full six feet. Gracie Davis looked formidable. She proceeded to pull the pistol from its holster, check that the safety was on, and then carefully replaced the gun in its holster. She then pulled on her jacket and placed the hat gingerly on her head so as to not ruin her hair. She could have been preparing for a dress parade.

From the trunk of the car she lifted a cooler, and then walked with ease to Edie and Phil's front door.

Edie answered the knock. "Gracie, you didn't have to get dressed up for us." She had been watching her friend's performance from the picture window.

"I did it for these backwater crackers, never know what they might do. Wanted them to know from the start who they were dealing with," said Gracie.

"They do now. This little burg will be talking about you for weeks. By the way," Edie said, pointing to the doorbell, "we do have one of those newfangled doorbells."

"Didn't know this bump in the road was so advanced, but when I know that babies are in the house, I knock," Gracie said, stepping into the house and setting the cooler down.

Phil, with Hillary in his arms, stopped on his way to the kitchen to greet Gracie. "Thanks for keeping Hillary and me company tonight. Did you bring food?"

"Yes. Give me that baby and take this stuff to the kitchen."

Edie gave Gracie a tour of the house finishing in the kitchen.

"Cozy house, this must be your favorite room," said Gracie.

"Good guess. It is," said Edie.

"Wasn't a guess. The baby's stuff is in here. Books and newspapers are scattered around the room. Chairs are pulled near the stove. The view is nice."

Edie looked at the room from Gracie's perspective; this is the room that they lived in. The other rooms were utilitarian, but this room with its expansive views and a wood stove was the best. This was where they gathered.

"I'll need a raise soon, we're going to have to buy that view someday," said Edie.

Gracie ignored the comment and turned her attention to the kitchen, where Phil was taking food out of the cooler.

"What a treat, your company and your food," said Phil. "Why'd you bring so much?"

"I've tasted your cooking," Gracie said as she read the instructions on the fridge. "Edie, are these commandments or suggestions on childcare that you have taped on this fridge?"

"Strict guidelines for Phil."

"Good, because I haven't forgotten how to mother these little ones," said Gracie, smiling at Hillary. Hillary returned the smile. "Phil, stop munching on those cookies, they'll spoil your dinner."

Phil shoved the rest of the cookie into his mouth, and then wiped the cookie crumb evidence from his face.

"Take this baby and go to the living room, I want to talk with Edie. See that you support her head and back," said Gracie, slow to hand the baby to Phil.

Edie smiled as she watched Phil clamp his mouth shut. He knew how to hold and care for a baby, he'd been doing it for two months, Phil retreated to the living room with his daughter.

Gracie focused on Edie. "What are your plans for tonight?"

"Same as it was for the last two Saturdays, canvass State Street. But with these photos, I might get somewhere." Edie spread the photos she had pulled from her pump bag on the counter. "Ian," she pointed to his photo, "was with this man last night at the Berger football game. I remembered where I'd seen him. State Street."

"Interesting development. Something I can throw to the bigwigs so they'll stop chewing my ass. Have you called Fred?" asked Gracie. "Or are you going alone?"

"I haven't called Fred, don't have any information to give him. Yes, I'm going alone. I think these college kids may remember more, if it was just me."

"Don't be stupid. You are not a lone ranger, and these are young people not kids you are dealing with," said Gracie.

"Ask her about her gun and cell phone," Phil shouted from the living room. "Then check them."

Edie looked exasperated. She didn't need advice from Phil on how to do her job. She could handle herself.

Gracie held out her hand. "Is his the voice of experience?"

Edie, after digging through the pump bag, handed Gracie the pistol.

Gracie checked that the safety was on, and then pulled the clip, it was full of bullets. She handed the gun back to Edie. "Now, your cell."

Edie patted her pockets, rummaged through the diaper bag and finally remembered that it was in her bedroom.

Gracie flipped it open, and then handed it back to Edie, "Low battery and this is your personal phone. You should be carrying the one provided by the department."

Edie went to retrieve it. She turned it on. Low battery.

"Phil, get your butt in here," Gracie called from the kitchen.

Phil obeyed. With a house filled with cops, did he have a choice?

"What would you like, ma'am?" Phil asked.

"Plug these cells in. Is your cell charged?"

"Yes."

"Give it to me, I need to put my work number in it. Also, I'm carrying it until Edie gets home." Gracie turned her attention to Edie. "You will carry my work phone tonight. Use it, if needed. Answer it when it rings. Don't ignore it."

"I'd never do that," said Edie.

"That's what my daughters tell me. I doubt them, too."

"What if it's the department?"

"Answer it, but that probably won't happen, I'm not the administrator on duty this weekend, but I'll give dispatch Phil's number, just in case."

Phil kept his back to Edie as he plugged in the phones. If he looked at her, he would make an I-told-you-so face at her and he would laugh. It was wonderful to have Gracie around. Maybe she could whip Edie into shape.

Edie closed the door behind her, grateful for the quiet of the night. She could handle either Gracie or Phil, but the two of them ganging up on her, that was a tough one. She didn't know which one of them to take down first. A smile spread across her face as she thought of Gracie using her commanding charm on Phil. She would whip him into shape, fast.

Edie stood in the middle of the road at the top of State Street. People stared at her, she didn't care. This night she did not want to disappear into the crowd. The street was busy. The Civic Center lights shown bright; one of the Broadway shows must be in town. It was the last home football game before Freak Fest brought thousands of kids to the State Street scene. The undulating stream of people created a logjam, first at the intersection at State and Johnson and again at State and Gorham. Next week, instead of football fans, there would be thousands of kids from around the Midwest taking over the street. Tonight would be Edie's best, but hopefully not her last, chance at finding the connections that could solve Russell Washington's murder.

The blare of a horn from a city bus brought Edie out of her thoughts. She joined the stream of people on the sidewalk and continued on her journey.

The Burger Joint was packed. Edie wondered if it exceeded code. She elbowed and shoved her way to the bar. Mallory was still sitting where Edie last saw her. Did Mallory ever leave the place?

"You're still here?" said Edie.

"Every Friday and Saturday night," replied Mallory.

"Thought you were a waitress."

"I am, if it's slow."

"What do you do here?"

"I'm more of a troubleshooter. Help out the waiters, the bartenders, keep an eye out for trouble. I try to keep this craziness from spinning out of control."

"Tia or Nola working tonight? I've got some new photos to show them."

"They're covering the back room. Can I see those photos?"

Edie pulled the photos from her pump bag. Mallory handed them back and shook her head no, she'd never seen them. Edie put them back in her bag, and then pushed, shoved, and elbowed her way to the back room.

Tia was taking an order; Nola was helping clear a table. Edie tried Nola first. A group of four waiting for the table Nola was clearing glared at Edie as she showed Nola the pictures. "Nope," said Nola, "none of them ring a bell."

Edie spotted Tia elbowing her way out of tight squeezes and make it to the bar. Edie pushed her way back to the main room to join Tia at the bar.

"Want me to arrest those guys?" asked Edie.

"Thanks, but I can handle those quick–feel guys. It's the wandering hands that need to be thrown out. What can I do for you?"

Edie pulled out the photos. "Recognize anyone?"

"Sorry, no. I gotta get back, can't leave Nola in there by herself."

Edie put one arm in front of her and the other on her bag as she shoved her way to the door. A hand on her shoulder caused Edie turn. Someone was about to be arrested. It was Mallory; she motioned to Edie to follow her outside.

Mallory took a deep breath. "Thanks for coming out with me. I needed some fresh air. Can I see those photos again?"

Edie handed them to her. Mallory stopped at one.

"This one brings back memories of me and Tim. He could be Tim's brother," Mallory said, handing the photos back to Edie.

"Does this Tim have a last name? And how do you know him?"

"Tim Esser. Met him at the county fair when we both showed animals, dated him for a while."

"Anything else? Did you ever meet this kid brother?"

"A few times at the fair. Back then he was just Tim's kid brother. Didn't pay much attention to him. I remember that boy would never leave us alone, tagged after Tim all the time. He was probably sent by his mother to chaperone us."

Edie put the photos back in her bag. "Remember his name?"

"No."

"Thanks, at least I've got something to go on."

Edie continued down State, went into three bars and came out with nothing except beer on her clothes. She stood in the middle of the sidewalk, trying to decide which bar to go into next, causing the crowd to part, then regroup beyond her. She felt an arm drop on her shoulder and the smell of beer wafted past her nose. She stomped on the person's foot; it was a man's shoe. She jabbed her elbow into his ribs and followed that thrust with the weight of her body, sending the guy backward. She shifted, jammed her knee into his groin, grabbed a thumb, and twisted.

"Uncle! Uncle!" shouted Mark Uselman. "Edie, let go of my thumb. I need it to work. And let up on the other part. I was hoping to use that tonight, too."

Some of the women on the street who had seen the action shouted their approval as they passed by. Edie released Mark, her reporter friend, then stood up.

Mark sat up. For a guy who worked out regularly, getting pushed to the ground had made him sore.

"Don't ever do that again," said Edie.

"Don't have to worry about that. What did you do that for?"

"Natural reaction. Why didn't you just say hi?"

"Thought we were friends."

"Friends announce themselves."

"What are you doing in Madison?"

"I'd ask you the same, but I can smell what you've been doing."

"Back at you."

"The beer's on my clothes, not my breath."

"This isn't your normal beat, so what are you doing down here?"

"Working."

"I'd heard—"

"Not here."

Edie extended a helping hand to Mark; he got up on his own. They walked to Peace Park, a few blocks away, found a place to sit away from the others. Edie and Mark watched the crowd as they continued their conversation in whispers.

"I'd heard you were working the Washington case," said Mark.

"You heard correctly."

"What can you tell me?"

"Nothing," said Edie.

"I got beat up for nothing? Police brutality."

"I'm thinking of pressing assault charges."

"Draw."

"What do you know?" Edie asked.

"Nothing. Strangest story I've worked. Nothing coming from the cops and nothing coming from the street. You got your work cut out."

"I'm finding that. Call me if you find anything?"

"Sure. And you me?"

Edie stood up, gave Mark a smile as she walked away, melting back into the crowd.

Nada. Nada. Nada. She was coming up with nothing. She should have stayed home. What she needed was to get out of the cold and the crowds. The Wayfarers Coffee House looked open. There were a few die–hard scholars with books propped in front of them.

She ordered a decaf caramel latte. Warmth and a surge of energy would do her good right now. Edie found a seat, one table back from the window. She warmed her hands around the cup and wished she was at Carole's with a cup of her winter special. This would have to do for tonight.

As she sipped her decaf and waited for her fingers to thaw, Edie watched the passing parade. State Street never disappointed, there was always something to see, the trendy stores, but mostly it was the people that Edie enjoyed watching. Like the man she saw walking on the other side of State Street, she put him above forty-five years old. He stopped to talk with one of the sweet young things hanging around the corner near the Stop and Rob. Edie couldn't take her eyes off of them. The girl leaned toward the man, then slid her arm through his. They crossed State Street together, fixated on each other. They walked past The Wayfarer's Coffee House The man was smiling. The girl was chatting. Edie's attention settled on the girl. Too much makeup for a young girl, good clothes, she was clinging tightly to the man's arm, then it hit Edie—she was one of the girls from the mall, one of the girls who would have robbed her as she shopped. And she was on State Street. Edie guessed that the girl had picked up a new trade, but tonight that wasn't her business. Edie was looking for information. A break in the Washington case.

When her fingers were finally able to move, Edie took the photos from the bag and stared at them. No use, they weren't talking. And neither was anyone else. She laid the photos on the table and turned her attention to the passing parade.

The barista cleaning the table next to Edie's cleared her throat.

Edie looked at her. "Is it closing time already?"

"No, I saw that picture on your table and wanted to get a closer look."

Edie handed her the pictures. The barista took them into a brighter light.

"It's a little fuzzy, but I think that looks like Devin."

"Is he a regular?"

"No, he's a drop–in. When he needs money, he drops in to work. Shawn lets him do odd jobs around here. Shawn's the owner, he likes to help people down on their luck, says it's dharma and it improves his chances with karma. Or something like that. I think Shawn's been in Madison too long."

"What do you know about Devin?"

"Nice guy, but one of those weirdoes who should have stayed in the woodwork."

"Does Devin have a last name?"

The barista yelled to the counter barista, "What's Devin's last name?"

"King or Miller. He's says he answers to both. I assume it's a hyphenated name."

"Do you know where he hangs out?"

"No clue. I've told you all I know," said the barista. "If you're done with that cup, I'll take it for you."

Edie handed her the half–filled cup, shoved the photos back into the bag, and floated on air to her car.

Most of the cars on the top deck were gone, but she didn't care. The Capitol lights shone bright, the holiday lights on the State Street trees were sparkling, what a wonderful night. She had a name. No, she had two names. Then she stopped. Her gut was trying to tell her something. She learned during her years as a beat cop to never overrule her gut. She twirled around and saw a couple coming out of the stairwell. They walked to their car. Edie got into hers and locked the door. She saw nothing, but she never overruled her gut. And it was telling her something wasn't right.

27

✳

Daylight came too early. Edie placed a pillow over her head to block the sun, but she couldn't escape the smells of breakfast. Food, that she didn't have to cook herself, was waiting for her in the kitchen.

Gracie handed Edie a mug of coffee as she made her way to the wood stove. Gracie followed with a plate of eggs, bacon, and cinnamon toast, which she placed on a chair next to Edie.

Gracie sat down, waiting for Edie to become functional.

"Where's Hillary?"

"In her crib, asleep," said Gracie.

"No one woke me."

"Phil said you got in late. I gave Hillary a bottle. Your brain functioning yet?"

"Another cup of coffee might do it. Where's Phil?" said Edie, holding out her mug to Gracie.

"He's catching up on some work in the shop."

While Gracie filled the mug, Edie ate.

The hunger was gone, but not the food. Edie relaxed and stretched her legs toward the stove.

"What did you find last night?" asked Gracie.

"That I'm old," said Edie. "Partying all night doesn't seem like fun anymore."

"I want to know about police business."

"And I thought you were interested in my welfare. The unknown boy has got a name, Ted Esser. The man's name is either Devin King or Devin Miller, goes by both, or it's hyphenated. He's a street person."

"Good start. What's your next move?"

"Run the names, see if there's anything in the files."

"When will you call Fred?"

"Tomorrow morning," said Edie.

"Today would be better."

"It's Sunday, even the FBI has to take a rest."

"Not when it involves one of their own. This is the first break we're getting. Share it with Fred TODAY."

"Can I let him have a quiet morning?"

"That's reasonable. You awake enough to care for this baby? I need to get back to my own family."

"I'm awake. It's nice having you here. Can I talk you into staying longer?"

"Sorry, this woman's work is never done. I've got a feast to prepare for my own family this afternoon."

At noon she called Fred; he said that he would run the names. She left a message on Steve's phone that she would like another meeting tomorrow at the office. The rest of her police work would wait until the morning when she went to the office.

The rest of the day belonged to Edie and Hillary. They spent it being warmed by the wood stove as they watched the farmers hurry to bring in the last of their crops. The combine went up the field, and then down it until the cornstalks were gone. A few deer were scared out of the field ahead of the combine. The combine emptied its yellow grains into a cart, and then returned to its rounds. It was mesmerizing. And when bedtime came, having spent the day in their pajamas, they were ready for it.

28

✳

Edie and Steve met first thing Monday morning.

"It seems you're stirring the pot," said Steve.

"I hoped to. What are you seeing?"

"Edginess, nothing concrete that kids want to confide in us—yet. It's like they are tiptoeing around everyone, not a good sign. Thanks for the tip about Eric Theis."

"What did he do to get your attention?"

"Nothing, but the kids that did talk to us clammed up when his name was mentioned. Tells me a lot. We'll have to make him one of our special projects."

"Good luck with that. His parents seem to have money and connections. He's off–limits to me, can only talk to the kid when their lawyer is present."

"In that case, we'll make him a priority. Kids that cocooned usually make their own reality and impose it on others."

Edie glued her butt to her chair and brought her case report up to date.

She reviewed the older parts of the report; no new connections jumped out at her. She looked through her inbox. There, near the bottom of the pile, was the toxicology report on Russell Washington. Edie jumped out of her chair and headed for the crime lab. The other cops in the room opened a path for her, and then closed rank and followed her. Some guessed that there was going to be a catfight and started to bet on the winner.

Sadie Carpenter was at her desk. She looked up when she heard the door hit the wall. Edie Swift had come to visit. In an apparent foul mood, as usual. Sadie squared her shoulders and returned to her work.

"What the fuck is this about?" said Edie, throwing the tox report on Sadie's desk.

Sadie picked up the paper, looked it over. "It's the toxicology report on Russell Washington."

"I can read. Why wasn't this put directly in my hands?"

"The report came back late Friday. You were gone."

"You should have sent me a memo."

"You should update yourself on your case," said Sadie, as she stood.

The women were eyeball–to–eyeball. No one in the department was brave enough, or dumb enough, to separate them. Fred Price did that for them.

"Edie, thought I'd come early for our meeting," said Fred, facing both combatants.

Edie nodded toward Fred, took a step away from Sadie, and in the distance saw money exchange hands among the deputies. Edie guessed that bets had quickly been placed on the confrontation between her and Sadie. She wondered who had won—her or Sadie, or was it a draw? "Let's go back to my desk, Fred."

Fred smiled at Sadie, "Thanks for e-mailing me the toxicology report." He took Edie's arm and guided her to Gracie's office.

Fred and Gracie let Edie fume for a few moments. "Ran the names and faces through our databases, nothing came up. I take it nothing came up on yours?" said Fred, when Edie had calmed down.

"Not even a driver's license," said Edie.

"Either he's from out of state or he doesn't have one, or Devin Miller, aka Devin King, has other aliases."

"The toxicology report explains a lot. Alcohol I expected, but I didn't think of flunitrazepam. That helps explain a few things."

"Every other test is clean. We have to step up our game," said Fred.

"Best place to push is those kids," said Gracie. "Edie, arrange a visit to the Victor Berger High School. Go in uniform and drive a marked squad. That should get some attention from those kids."

"Any suggestions on how to shake things up, besides that?" Edie asked.

"You're working the case, come up with something," said Gracie.

Fred and Edie left Gracie's office together.

"Feels like we're punting here," said Fred. "I'll work the drug angle. What are you going to do?"

"Go back to high school," said Edie as she escorted him to the elevators. "I may need your clout with one of the families."

"Which one?"

"The LeRoy and Madonna Theis family."

"Call me anytime. This lawman will ride to your rescue anytime, except when you're stuck in line to get out of a parking ramp."

Edie ignored his little jab. "Can you run the Theis family through your databases?"

"Yes. You think I'll find something?"

"I doubt it, probably confirm that they are connected and they don't mind rubbing my nose in it."

"Sounds like I should pay them a visit," said Fred.

"I got this one covered for now, thanks. Keep me informed," said Edie as the elevator doors closed on Fred. But Edie wasn't certain that she had it covered.

Edie went back to her desk, and reviewed her case report. It was solid. The flunitrazepam added a new twist, but explained others. Better known on the streets as roaches, R2, roofies, wolfies, and other tags used to define 'us versus them', the names were an act of demarcation; its side effects ranged from drowsiness to retroactive amnesia with death thrown in. Flunitrazepam explained how an experienced agent was taken—but not the fury of the attack, nor the why. For Edie, the case, though clearing, was still fuzzy. She cleared her desk and went home.

In theory, being at home should have given Edie space to view the problem from a different angle. It didn't. She was inundated with more work.

She cleaned the kitchen counter, ran the dishwasher, put diapers in the washer to soak, folded the dry ones, and put the newspapers in the recycling bin. Edie needed relief from more work. Home was supposed to be about relaxation. Today it wasn't. She put Hillary in the front pouch, put on Phil's heavy winter coat, and walked down to his shop.

It didn't help. Phil was busy, he couldn't talk. For a while Edie watched him work on one of his trucks, and then left. She walked through Troutbeck; there was nothing new to distract her. She looked at the church with its cemetery, she didn't want anything that quiet. Edie went back home.

That night, when Phil walked in the door, Hillary was dumped in his arms.

"Your supper's on the counter. I need a run," said Edie as she left.

Edie knew it was better to run in town during an autumn night. She jogged toward Troutbeck proper. She jogged in place in the shadow of the vacant store to block the western wind. The number of cars driving past the Halloween house seemed to have increased. For a moment she thought of volunteering to take down the decorations. Edie continued to jog in place, waiting for a break in the traffic. A Lexus caught her eye. She did a double-take when she recognized its driver. Jake Thomas. What the hell was he doing in her neighborhood? She passed up the opportunity to sprint across the road as Thomas's car crawled past the Halloween house; she wanted to see where he was going without being noticed herself. Once past the house, the car picked up speed and farther down the road turned back toward the main highway. Strange. Maybe she needed to interview Jake Thomas again. But she'd think about that later.

She ran up and down the same short streets. In the past, the repetitiveness of running freed her mind to work on problems. This time it didn't work. She knocked on Carole's door, jogging in place as she waited for a response.

"I need a haircut," said Edie when Carole finally opened the door.

"Nice to see you, too. You just had a haircut," said Carole. "But come on in anyway."

Edie followed her to the salon.

"Should I charge you for therapy or a style?" Carole asked.

"Thought you said it was one and the same? What I need is some neutral space to think about this case. I came home this morning to get a change of scenery. In the past, ideas about a case would pop up if I focused on something else. But I walked into my house and my brain filled with Hillary's needs. Everything else was pushed out of my mind. I think my brain is turning to mush."

"That's normal, you're a mother. So what do you want me to do?"

"Something to get me out of myself, someplace where I'm not thinking of Hillary. Running didn't help. Sex hasn't helped. How about a hairwash and a style?"

"That I can do. Put it on your tab?"

"Yeah," Edie said as the warm water soaked her hair. For the first time that day she relaxed. And her mind wandered.

Carole kicking her out of the salon brought Edie to the here and now. The pieces of the case were falling into place, but there was no evidence. It was all conjecture, nothing concrete, barely even circumstantial. But she felt better. The case felt like it was moving forward, not at a standstill.

29

✳

At work, preparations for Freak Fest were in the final stages. Deputies signed up for extra shifts to help the city and campus police. Weather reports were carefully watched; some deputies hoped for rain to keep the crowds down, while others hoped for unseasonal warm weather so they wouldn't freeze their asses. Edie was oblivious. She'd done her share of work during Halloween celebrations on State Street. This year she smiled as she declined the offers, for she was on maternity leave, sort of.

Today, Edie's problem was Mr. and Mrs. Theis. More precisely, she couldn't get near their son, and she wasn't coming up with a solution to that. Edie let that problem dangle. Something would come to mind, soon, she hoped.

Instead, Edie arranged a meeting with Patricia Boehnen and Ian at school with Principal Zander in attendance. Edie would pick her up at ten. That left an hour to kill. A leisurely drive out to the Boehnens would be nice, thought Edie.

Edie got to the Boehnen farm earlier than anticipated. So she drove past the Boehnen farm to the Theis farm. She had plenty of time to talk with that family.

The farmyard was still immaculate. Edie wondered how they did it. Not a leaf was on the yard, no cornstalks from neighboring farms littered the lawn. The earth tones of her squad car made a nice natural addition to the lawn. It was easily visible through the denuded flora. Just to make sure that passing drivers would see the car, she left the car where the driveway began. Slowly, she emerged from the car, stretched, made sure her weapons were in place and hoped that every neighbor was watching. Living on a hill was an enigma. You set yourself away from everyone, but everyone could see you, always—maybe that was the plan.

Her knock was answered by Mrs. Theis.

"Get your car off from my property," Mrs. Theis greeted Edie.

"I only have a few questions."

"If you want to talk to me, you will move your car off my property," said Mrs. Theis, closing the door on Edie.

Edie ambled back to her car, idled the car in the driveway checking, several times, for road traffic before she backed onto the road. The driver coming down the hill laid on the horn as she swerved to miss Edie's car. Edie parked in the ditch in front of the Theis home and walked back to the house.

Mrs. Theis answered the door, with Mr. Theis behind her.

"I asked you to move your car," said Mrs. Theis.

"And I complied with that request. My squad is parked in the ditch, a public right of way. I'm hoping to persuade you folks to let me talk to your son."

"Didn't you get the message?" asked Mrs. Theis.

"What message is that, ma'am?"

"You are off the case."

"No, ma'am, my boss did not relay that order to me. Fact is, I was requested to take this case."

Mrs. Theis was checked. She turned to her husband. "Roy, what do we do now?"

"We thank the deputy for her interest, tell her that we and our son are off–limits, according to our lawyer. And, if she wants information, to call our lawyer." He shook hands with Edie. "Thank you, next time you come to our home, bring someone with more authority with you."

"I will, the FBI," Edie said to the closed door.

Edie was left standing on the porch, smiling.

Timing is everything, Edie reminded herself, as she sat in the squad in front of the Victor Berger High School with Patricia Boehnen in the passenger seat. When Edie wasn't looking at her watch, she was looking at her cell phone, all the while talking with Mrs. Boehnen.

"Excuse me, it's time we went in," said Edie, getting out of the car and putting on her hat.

Patricia Boehnen, puzzled by the delay, followed. The women were buzzed into the school and met by Principal Zander.

"Hope you don't mind waiting a few moments. The bell is going to ring shortly, and I like to be in the hall between classes. Gives the students the idea that I'm approachable," said Principal Zander.

"Not at all," said Edie. "Hope you don't mind me standing here either." Edie took a position next to Principal Zander. Edie handed her briefcase to Patricia Boehnen, who was left to her own devices. With her hat on, one hand on her gun, Edie stood tall and alert.

It seemed to Edie that the students were quieter than usual. Some of them hurried past her, some kept their heads down, but few walked past her alone. All the students looked like they were running a gauntlet. Edie was certain that she would be the talk of the lunchroom and, hopefully, the rest of the day.

After requesting that Ian Boehnen be called to her office, Principal Zander indicated that Edie and Patricia Boehnen should follow her.

This time, Edie found the sparse room relaxing. There was nothing to distract her. The women waited quietly for Ian.

Ushered into the office, Ian flashed a smile at his mother as he sat in the chair next to her.

"Ian," Edie began. "Do you remember me? I'm Detective Swift. I've got a few photos that I'd like you to see." She opened her briefcase and handed the photos of Ted Esser, Eric Theis, and Devin Miller, aka King, to him. "Do you recognize anyone?"

As Edie watched, Ian studied them. She noticed Ian's eyes widened as he recognized the people.

"Yeah," Ian said as he handed the photos one by one back to Edie. "This one is Ted Esser, this one is Eric Theis, and I don't know who this one is." Ian kept his eyes on the floor.

"Could you keep them and show them to your friends?" asked Edie.

Ian looked up for a moment as he took the photos from Edie, then returned his gaze to the floor.

"Thanks," said Edie. "If anyone recognizes the older man, please call me." She handed Ian another business card.

Zander broke the silence. "Any more questions for Ian, Detective Swift?"

"No."

"Then, Ian, you may go back to class. Stop at the front desk for a hall pass," said Principal Zander.

Patricia Boehnen followed her son to the outer office.

Principal Zander studied Edie for a moment. "Was bringing Mrs. Boehnen to this meeting necessary?"

"Yes."

"Was this a show of force? Does this have anything to do with the increased gang education in the community? And do I need to know any more?"

"I certainly hope not," said Edie. "What can you tell me about Sean Coyle?"

"Nothing," said Principal Zander.

"What can you tell me about Ted Esser?"

"Nothing."

"What can you tell me about Eric Theis?"

Zander hesitated, stared at the floor for a moment, raised her head, met Edie's stare. "Nothing."

"Thank you for your time." Edie shook Zander's hand then left. Zander's moment of silence spoke volumes to Edie. She wondered if, with all her diplomas, Zander understood hers.

Edie drove Patricia Boehnen back to her farm. Patricia hesitated before leaving the car. "Did you really need me there today?"

Edie sat quiet.

"Do you think my son is in trouble?"

Edie felt sorry for this mother; she wanted to step away from her job and speak to Patricia Boehnen, mother to mother. Edie wanted to tell her that Ian should be grounded for life, he should wear a tracking device, and he should never leave his mother's sight. But she didn't. Edie hoped that today's performance would force someone into the open; she hoped that the Boehnens could read between the lines. Instead, Edie said to Patricia Boehnen, "Mrs. Boehnen, I don't know if your son is in trouble. A terrible crime happened at Indian Lake. I think some of the boys aren't telling me everything they know about that night. I don't know if your son is one those boys. But it is my job to find the people who did it. And I will." Patricia Boehnen did not need to know anything else, thought Edie. Each of us will have to play whatever hand is dealt. Edie watched as a deflated Patricia Boehnen got out of the squad.

She hoped that tomorrow's meeting with the Coyles would go better.

30

*

E die heard the knock, and then the door open. Damn, we forgot to lock the door, again. She heard Mrs. Voss call out.

"Anyone home?"

For a moment, Edie thought of staying silent or maybe yelling "just us burglars," but she didn't. "I'm changing Hillary; we'll be out in a moment."

When they came into the living room, Mrs. Voss extended a plate of decorated Halloween cookies to Edie.

"I made cookies for my family. Thought I'd decorate some for you and Phil."

Edie took the plate from Mrs. Voss, and then handed her Hillary. "They look beautiful!"

"My kids say that too, and then complain I never did these things when they were little. But I don't see them doing it for their little ones now. Guess they're learning how busy parents are." Mrs. Voss began swaying as Hillary nestled in her arms.

Edie stood in the kitchen doorway, watching Hillary fall asleep. "Can you watch Hillary for a bit? I don't want to disturb her and I'd like to take a run." Edie didn't wait for response; she went to her room to change into running gear. Mrs. Voss was already settled into the glider when Edie returned. "Here's my cell number, if you need me."

Edie headed north into farm country. The leaves were gone from the trees except the oaks, which would hold on to them even during the coming winter storms. Stubble was all that was left in some of the fields. The brilliant autumn blue sky had dimmed to a pale blue. The world seemed to be shutting down. And the wind carried the scent of Arctic air. Edie felt the urge to pick up her pace, but running marathons taught her to keep to her pace.

A mile into the run Edie reached the crossroads. She jogged in place as she considered the merit of each route: around the block with its hills or straight north into country she had never run. She chose north. It was country she wanted to see, but had been too busy to explore when she first moved to Troutbeck, until today. It was open farmland, except for the seven houses huddled together, almost the beginnings of a Wisconsin town. Empty brown fields were checker-boarded with green fields. The fields to the west ended in a marsh. To the east were more farm fields defined by fence rows made of barbed wire and trees.

Edie's run stopped at the river. She turned around and headed back home. She felt as if the world was hers and hers alone, until she looked up. A bald eagle was circling above her and a turkey vulture was sitting in the oak at the river's edge. She was not alone, and she understood that she could only do what she could do. No superheroes to the rescue, there were no do-overs in this world. You picked the way through whatever was thrown in your way, to the best of your ability. She knew all that, it was one of her mantras when she started a new case, but couldn't this case be the exception?

The run did her good; it was possible, she thought, that she could face one more family in denial. She dressed for the Coyle interview.

The drive to the Coyle farm was unbearable, almost. Edie had been over this road so many times in the last few weeks, the car seemed to be on autopilot. She even waved at Madonna Theis, who acknowledged the wave with a one-finger salute.

The Coyle farm was on the other side of the town, around a few hills, past a couple of bars and a church, then into open country. The second farm on the left, you can't miss it, it's the only farm on the road that has a Century Farm sign on it were the directions she was given at the gas station in town.

Edie did miss it.

She turned around on a field road and backtracked a quarter of a mile.

Stepping out of her car she saw a mass of redheads coming toward her.

The older woman of the group introduced herself as she wiped her hands on her blue jeans and thrust one toward Edie. "I'm Erin Coyle. Sorry, my husband Niall couldn't be here. Hope you don't mind a little dirt, we're cleaning up, the cows are being sold tomorrow. One of them kicked Niall, now he wants all of them off his farm." The mass of younger redheads lined up behind their mother. "These are our kids: Dylan, Quinn, Liam, Maeve, Keeva. Now, does anyone know where that black Irish kid is?"

No one admitted to knowing where he was.

"Well, he's around the place," said Erin Coyle. "Now, what can we do for you, officer?"

"Let me introduce myself first. I'm Detective Swift. Can we talk alone?"

"Can't hide anything from these kids, they'll tease it out of me later or make up fantastic stories about it. Since lies spread faster than truths, better if they hear what we say for themselves."

"I'd like to ask Sean some questions about a certain Saturday night he spent with friends."

"I'm guessing it's about that troublemaker Eric Theis."

"Don't know about that. I'd like to talk with Sean and hear what he has to say."

"I should have thrown that brat off the farm the first day I met him."

"That's what we told you to do, Ma," said Maeve.

"That was then, this is now. Sean!" Erin Coyle yelled. "Sean!"

A black–haired boy came out of the house. Edie guessed it was Sean Coyle. How did a black–haired kid get mixed in with all these redheads, she asked herself.

"He has the look of my grandfather, he was a black Irishman too; sweetest man to walk the face of the earth. Don't know why everyone thinks all Irish are redheads," Erin Coyle said, smiling at her son.

"That's not what your mother says," said Dylan, taking two giant steps out of his mother's reach.

Erin Coyle eyed Detective Edie Swift, before ignoring Dylan. "Sean, come over here. This detective has some questions for you."

Sean walked over to his family, slowly.

"Sean," Edie started. "I've been told that you hang out with Ian Boehnen a lot."

"A sweet young man," said Erin Coyle.

"He's one of my friends," said Sean, looking at the ground.

"Were you with him the night of the incident at Indian Lake Park?"

"Which incident are you talking about?" Quinn Coyle asked.

"The night of the murder," answered Edie as she watched Sean for a reaction. She wasn't going to be misdirected from her purpose by anyone.

"I was with Ian and Ted and Eric that night," Sean answered immediately, still looking at the ground.

"I remember that night, I stayed up to ask you some questions about my math homework and the parents were mad at me the next morning because I slept through my chores and they had to do them," said his sister Keeva.

"You were home early, at least before midnight," said Dylan. "I know, because I needed to be in bed by midnight that night and I saw Sean before I went to bed."

Edie looked at the bunch of them as they circled around their brother to protect him. "Is that right, Sean?"

"Yes, ma'am," said Sean.

"Do you remember what you and your friends did that night?" quizzed Edie.

"We went to Madison, to the mall."

"Yes, I asked him to pick up some sports socks for me," said Liam.

Edie looked at the family. All for one, one for all. Admirable attitude for a family to have, Edie thought. She saw that she wasn't going to get anything out of Sean—or his family. "Thank you for your time. It was very informative." Edie shook hands with each of the Coyles before getting into her car.

Erin Coyle saw her off. "May the road rise with you."

"No, Ma, that was last week's blessing," said Keeva.

"Then what's this week's blessing?"

"If God sends you down a stony path, may he give you strong shoes," said Quinn.

"And we send you off with that blessing," said Erin Coyle as Edie started her car.

The Coyle family waved her out of the farmyard.

In her rearview mirror, she saw Dylan and Quinn wrestle Sean to the ground, then Liam, Maeve, and Keeva take turns giving him a noogie, and Erin Coyle walk back to the barn after watching her family's torment of their brother.

Families, thought Edie, shaking her head. This one seemed to be one of the better ones. She was certain that Sean was lying. He had told her the exact same story Ian Boehnen had told her. But, still, she admired a family sticking up for one of their own. She imagined that the punishment Sean's brothers and sisters would hound him with would be a life sentence.

Edie was almost to Indian Lake Park when she started to pound on the steering wheel. She pulled over onto the shoulder, rammed the gears into park, and continued to pound the steering wheel. "Damn it. Damn it. Damn it. Then Ian and Sean are either lying or they're not telling me all they know. They seem to be nice boys and I hope to high heaven that is the extent of their involvement. Damn it. I didn't set this thing in motion. Somebody did, but not me! Russell Washington was killed. He needs justice. His family needs justice. Society is demanding it. I took on this work to help deliver it. I need to do my job. Damn." Edie didn't know where the reluctance to finish this case came from, but she shoved it aside. She wiped away the tears, let out a deep sigh, put her car into drive and continued on her journey.

Edie looked at her watch. It was late, she needed to pick up Hillary fifteen minutes ago. And tomorrow and Friday were going to be long days. She'd have to re-schedule the interview with Ted Esser and his family for Saturday.

She turned toward home.

31

✳

Thursday Edie cleaned the house. Vacuumed—twice. The bathroom corners were scrubbed, the kitchen cupboards were emptied, and wiped down. Edie was putting everything back into the cupboards when Phil came home.

"You pregnant?" Phil asked.

"I just got done being pregnant. Why would I do that again so soon?"

"Because the last time you cleaned the cupboards was the day before Hillary was born. If you're not nesting, why are you cleaning?"

"You want me to stop?" asked Edie.

"No, no . . . you just keep doing what you want," said Phil, walking out to the living room. He settled into the recliner and said softly, "All you need now is the *kirche*."

"I heard that," shouted Edie.

"No you didn't. Can you bring me a beer?"

"Here's your beer. I put another log on the fire, and I may not've heard what you said, but I can read your mind. Enjoy the beer, this will never happen again." Edie sat on the couch next to him. "I'm antsy because this case seems to be coming together, but not fast enough. I'm antsy because of the direction it seems to be taking. I'm antsy because of Freak Fest. The house is clean because I don't know what to do with all this energy. Carole won't touch my hair for another four weeks. Running doesn't help much."

Phil slid from his chair to kneel in front of Edie. "Maybe I can help you." His kisses started at her hands and continued upward until he brushed her hair from her face and pulled her to the floor. His hands slipped under her sweater. He could feel her abs tighten.

"Sorry. There's still some baby fat to lose."

Phil smothered her belly with kisses as his hands undid her bra, and then followed her curves south.

Edie and Phil lay together, spent. Phil slept on her breasts. One of her arms cradled him, the other floated down his back and beyond. It was a slender body and soft. The tranquility that Phil radiated masked an explosive power. Few people saw beyond the facade, they were lulled by that softness. He was like a cool night breeze after a hot summer's day. But he was anything but tranquil the day they met.

She had taken the call from dispatch. When she got to the incident, she saw a car smashed into a tree. The tree and car were goners. People were gathered around an older woman, comforting her. Between sobs about her grandfather's tree being ruined, and how could he do such a thing, and the man should be strung up, at least thrown in jail and the key thrown away, Edie was able to find that no one in that group was hurt. She went to check on the man in the car. She knocked on the window, there was no response. She opened the door, he fell out. The driver looked up, smiled, and in slurred speech said, "Did you drop from heaven just for me?" After that, he was out of control, all hands. He had the height and weight advantage, but Edie had experience with drunks and wrestled him to the ground, handcuffed him, placed him in the back of the squad. The family cheered. Edie drove him to detox.

Who'd a thunk they would end up together and with a baby? Not Edie.

"Enough of this reminiscing," Edie said, softly. "I've got a job to do."

Edie shifted her weight, Phil woke up.

"Where are you going?'

"State Street."

"How many times do you have to go there?"

"After tonight? Once . . . I hope."

"Stay and snuggle with me?"

"I can't. Duty calls."

"Sleep is calling too.'

"Not for me."

"Sex makes me sleepy. Why does it seem to energize women?"

"And how many women have you had that you know this?"

"Just you, Sweetie, just you."

Edie knelt beside him, and then kissed him. "Liar. Supper's in the oven. And the baby monitor is on the end table."

Edie parked in the Dayton Street ramp and headed down State Street. Tonight's assignment was to savor the street and the people who claimed it as their Main Street.

Edie looked for the stores she frequented as a student, most were gone. Styles and tastes and the stores followed whatever the trend of the day was. There were a few stores that had become timeless, the stores that had weathered the fickleness of style trends. Edie lingered at their storefronts.

But the crowds on State remained the same, Edie thought as she turned to watch the mass of people. The serious students' goal was to get to one of the campus libraries; they weren't distracted by any changing store's merchandise—that was until they reached the used bookstores. Then there were those students whose creed was that the weekend started Thursday night. This night some of students on the street had arrived early for Freak Fest, the early Halloween party that Madison hoped would control the number of kids on State and stop the bacchanal and destructive behavior of earlier years. There were a few shop owners who were busy rearranging their merchandise; they'd been through Freak Fest many times. And city workers were setting out barricades and high-intensity lights that would be put in place before Freak Fest.

A TV crew was setting up for a story. Edie stopped on Gorham Street to watch. Leigh Stone, when the setup was completed, stepped out of the news van. Edie Swift quickly moved to the other side of State in an attempt to blend in with the other curiosity seekers all asking themselves the same question: What brought a TV crew to State Street?

Edie could hear Leigh recap prior years' violence during Freak Fest, where traffic would be rerouted, the procedures for getting into the Fest—a public service announcement, how kind of her. Edie also saw Fred Price try to blend into the crowd that had gathered near the TV crew. As Leigh wrapped up her coverage, Edie moved on. She saw that Leigh Stone had recognized her, and was following her.

Edie heard Leigh Stone call her name. She turned up her coat collar, scrunched down inside it, and continued on. The tap on the shoulder finally stopped Edie. Edie turned around. It was Leigh Stone. Edie walked on. Leigh Stone fell in beside her.

"Detective Edie Swift, what are you doing on State Street? Does this have anything to do with the Indian Lake case?"

"Ms. Stone. I'm here as a private citizen. Leave me alone."

"Really? I'd heard you were back on the force."

"I was never off it."

"What can you tell me about the case?

"Nothing."

"The people have a right to know how that case is progressing."

"And they will; you should talk to Lieutenant Davis about that. But tonight, as I, only seconds ago, told you, I'm here as a private citizen."

"Mark says you're always on duty."

"Mark should mind his own business." Edie stopped, turned to face Leigh. She saw that Fred Price had disappeared from view. "Excuse me," said Edie, ducking into one of the fast–food restaurants. She hadn't meant to be so polite to Leigh Stone. Edie ordered a pop, sat near the window, and sipped until Leigh Stone gave up and walked away. Edie waited five more minutes, chucked the rest of her pop in the wastebasket and took the back streets to the Dayton Street ramp. It was a comfortable walk, knowing that Fred Price also thought answers to their case would be found on State

32

*

Freak Fest day came, and Edie was still debating whether or not to go in costume. Should she blend in or just go as herself? This wasn't her holiday. As a child, the only thing she liked about Halloween was the free candy. Even then she didn't like to scare anyone with ghosts, goblins, or ghouls. Nothing changed when she became an adult, except that now it was her job to protect against the real ghosts, goblins, and ghouls.

When Freak Fest opened for business, Edie was at her house, still trying to decide whether or not to wear a costume.

The traffic waiting to get into the Dayton Street ramp spilled out of North Carroll Street and on to Dayton. Edie waited in that line and then the next line inside the ramp that was hunting for a parking space. This time she vowed to park in any open area, legal or not.

Edie sat in her car on the top floor, trying to calm herself down. The wait to get into the ramp had been long. She hated waiting, and more so tonight. Tonight she didn't want to be surrounded by young people trying to get drunk or high. She wanted to get her job finished with.

She looked up to see Dorothy and Toto disappear through the stair door. It was time to join the revelers.

Halfway to the stairwell, Edie checked her pockets for her ticket into Freak Fest. It wasn't there. She went back and searched her car; it had slipped out of her pocket and was between the cushions of the driver's seat. This prompted her to check her other stuff. Her hat was on her head, gloves in her jacket pocket, her gun she shoved to the bottom of the glove compartment—she wouldn't need it, there were plenty of officers on duty. Locking the compartment and the car, Edie joined the crowds on the street waiting to get onto State Street.

The costumes distracted Edie as she waited. There were Holsteins, bananas, cheeses, Things 1&2, Union Terrace chairs, pregnant nuns, Waldos, Samanthas, Kirstens, Santa and his reindeer. Some of the costumes Edie thought she could use in later years for Hillary.

It was a shock to Edie that children were trick-or-treating on State Street. The small firemen with their Dalmatians, ladybugs, dinosaurs, giraffes were guided from shop to shop as the children marveled at grown-ups also in costume. Edie looked at her watch, it was time those parents took those children home.

A strong arm pulled Edie out of the way of the racing sausages. She jabbed her elbow into the person who had done that, heard him gasp, and then turned to see who it was. Deputy Johnson was doubled over, and Smith was with him, laughing.

"Seen anything yet?" asked Johnson as he struggled to stand up.

"No. I've been admiring the costumes; it must have taken them weeks to prepare those costumes."

"Nothing like the old days, is it, Ren?" Deputy Smith said. "When we were young, didn't need a costume. We went naked. Cops caught us shinnying up a street lamp. Buddies had to bring us clothes when they bailed us out."

"Don't remember that," said Johnson.

"Sure you do. It was the Halloween before the one when they took us to detox."

"Don't remember that one, either."

"And they let you two on the force?" said Edie. It was a night of revelations. "Have you seen anything?"

"Nope," Johnson and Smith said in unison.

Edie continued down the street. A wicked witch waved her broomstick at Edie, presumably sending a curse her way. A good witch dove to intercept the curse, and then touched Edie on the head with her wand as if to bless her. She turned to watch the good witch and the bad witch link arms and continue weaving their magic as they floated down State. "Damn, never thought they were collaborators," Edie said to no one in particular. Edie turned to see stars appear, bananas, a number of 'Screams', she wondered if Venus on the Half Shell, or Lady Godiva, or David would appear later, or was it too cold? Or had Freak Fest become tamer?

A guy with a huge blond afro walked past Edie with a woven belt circling his head, another keeping his bell bottom jeans above his skinny ass. A girl dressed in a long peasant skirt, embroidered blouse, combat boots, and rose-colored glasses held his hand. "Mom?" Edie whispered. *No, she thought, it couldn't be her. This girl was young ; how old would her mother be now? Fifty-five, sixty?*

Edie took a cleansing breath. The sweet, spicy aroma of weed was pulled into her lungs. It was the scent of her mother. Edie took a second deep breath, trying to determine which direction the scent was coming from. She looked at the burgeoning crowd, and at the student apartments above the State Street stores-the scent could be coming from anywhere. Edie wondered, as she continued down the street, if there had ever been a study on the effects of marijuana's secondhand smoke. Probably not, she thought, someone would have to admit that they inhaled.

Edie also noted that the street was well–lit; police were at all the intersections, some were walking the street.

As the cold deepened and the night darkened, the children were hustled home to bed and the street was left for the adults, or the so–called adults. Edie felt something warm trickling down her abdomen, she was leaking.

"Damn, I forgot my pump at home." She looked for a quiet place to express the milk, a bathroom where she could lock the door. If the breast pump made people squeamish, Edie didn't want to find out what the reaction would be to a woman manually expressing breast milk.

She ducked into The Wayfarer's Coffee House.

Edie was halfway up the stairs to the bathroom when the barista yelled to her, "Those are for customers."

"I'll be one shortly!" Edie yelled back.

Fifteen minutes later, Edie was at the counter ordering a hot chocolate to go. The barista took a sharp look at her; Edie's pupils weren't dilated or pinpoints. The barista decided it was okay to serve her.

"That shortly was on what timeline?"

"Eternity's. Seen Devin lately?" countered Edie.

"No."

Edie took her hot chocolate in a to–go cup. At the door she remembered her manners. "Thanks," she called back to the barista, and then joined the Halloween show.

The lines outside the bars grew longer. The crowd packed tighter. One drunk plowed into Edie. She put a defensive arm between the drunk and herself, but not before her hot chocolate erupted over her jacket. She brushed off what liquid she could; the jacket was probably a loss. She'd had enough of the crowd.

Side streets didn't look any less crowded. The crowds on one street looked to be at a standstill, but they were out of the swollen, pushing crowd. Edie headed for it. She joined the line to get into The Drunken Duck Inn. Maybe she could get a chair there.

It was a miracle; she got to the door after only thirty minutes of waiting. A bouncer told her there was a two–drink minimum. Edie decided she could hold that much hot chocolate or even pop if necessary. She was let in. The place was packed. On second thought, maybe this wasn't a good idea. Edie turned to go when someone fell into her. Edie braced herself against the momentum. If she fell in this place, she'd probably never get up. And her body wouldn't be found until after bar time, maybe. Then she felt liquid seeping down the inside of her jacket. Then she smelled it–beer. Then she heard it, a familiar voice. "Oh, I'm so sorry." Edie twisted around to face the offender.

Madonna Theis, dressed in a glittery white robe with sparkly iridescent wings and a golden halo. She was out of character, Edie thought.

"Oh, it's you," said Madonna Theis. "Now I'm sorry I didn't have more beer."

LeRoy Theis, dressed in his devil costume, pushed his way through the crowd with two beers in his hands. "Saw what happened, dear, brought you another one." He saw Edie standing next to his wife. "It's Ms. Swift. What a surprise. Are you following us? Do we have to get a restraining order against you?" He chugged his beer, then his wife's beer, put his arm around Madonna. "Let's get out of here; the place is attracting less–desirable clientele."

So this is Beelzebub's Lair, thought Edie. She didn't know she had fallen so far. Edie watched as Beelzebub and his disciple pushed through the crowd to the exit. The place was improving.

A chair in the window opened up. Edie won the race to it. She sat between a piece of the Berlin Wall and someone who, less creative than herself, had taped a sign identifying him as the White Cliffs of Dover. When a waitress accidentally wandered close to her, Edie ordered a hot chocolate.

The hot chocolate had cooled considerably by the time it got to Edie. She watched the street, sipped her drink, and felt herself relax.

"Excellent beginning. Excellent beginning to my holiday, isn't it, Ms. Swift?"

Edie turned toward the voice. Jake Thomas. She was wrong, the place hadn't gotten better when Lucifer left. Jake Thomas was here.

"Nice of you to remember," said Edie. Something about him was different. She looked closer. His lips were fuller. Edie fought to suppress a laugh.

"My wife says I have a memory for people; I don't know why I have that skill, I never cultivated it. She thinks it's natural, tells me that I should go into politics," said Jake Thomas.

"That could be an interesting line of work for you. What brings you downtown?"

"Reminiscing."

"You're not in costume?"

"I'm just remembering the good times I had when I first came to town, not reliving them. I'd talk longer, but my wife is expecting me at home. Nice to see you again."

He held out his hand to her and smiled. Edie shook it and watched as Jake Thomas made his way out of the bar and into the dark end of the street.

She turned her attention back to the bar in time to see Santa leading his reindeer to it. A hand from the crowd reached out to squeeze a reindeer's ass. The reindeer swung around and nailed the offender in the face. Santa turned, swinging his sack over his head, as he, too, charged at the offender. The Statue of Liberty went to intervene, but her torch was grabbed from her and used to club Santa. The Blues Brothers tried to sneak out of the bar, but got caught in the melee. Edie set her drink down and started toward the fight to break it up. The bouncers beat her to it. They pulled people out of the fight zone and threw them out the door; when one offender was thrown out, one person was let into the bar.

Edie admired the skill of the bouncers as they pulled people from the free–for–all and threw them out the door. Fights must be a regular occurrence, she thought. I'll have to pass this on to the Madison cops. Hopefully they already knew. With the fight under control, Edie returned to her seat between the rock and the hard place. Her hot chocolate was colder. She gulped the remaining liquid and stared at the costumed people waiting to get into the Drunken Duck.

Half an hour later Edie put her head on the window counter; she was tired, maybe it was the warmth of the bar that was doing it. Maybe fresh air would perk her up. Edie stumbled out of the bar. The fresh air didn't revive her. She sank to the pavement. Strong arms pulled her up and guided her toward the dark. She tried to wave the fog away to see who was helping her up.

"Such big eyes you have, Ms. Swift," the man said.

"You look familiar, do I know you?" Edie asked. Her voice sounded far away, as if disconnected from her body.

"We've met. I've been watching you."

Edie's vision blurred more. She planted her face in his, "I've seen you . . . you're . . . you're . . . it starts with a D."

"Devin."

Edie's memory ended there.

33

*

Phil rolled over in bed. Edie wasn't there to snuggle with. He reached back for the alarm clock. 12:30. Damn her, she said she'd be back by 11:30. He sat on the edge of their bed and punched Edie's number. He heard her phone ring in Hillary's room. Double damn her. He called Gracie. She hadn't heard from Edie, but Phil shouldn't worry, Edie could handle herself. She must have gotten a lead on her case. She'll be fine. They hung up. Phil knew Edie could handle herself, but he was hers; it was his right to worry.

At 1:00 a.m., Phil knocked on Sera Voss's door. It took time, but Sera Voss peeked through her front-window curtain. She opened the door with a flashlight in her hand.

"Phil, what's wrong?" she asked.

"Why are you assuming something's wrong?"

"Why are you knocking on my door after midnight?"

"Edie's not home. Can you come sit with Hillary?"

"Of course." Sera Voss went back to get her keys. She locked her door and followed Phil back to his house.

Phil told Sera where she could find everything, pointed out the instructions on the fridge, handed her Edie's cell, and pulled his winter work coat from the closet. He went to the basement, pulling his .30–06 rifle from the gun safe, just in case. It was also his right to go find Edie.

34

❋

Phil pulled into the Doty Street ramp. Since it was pretty much empty he was able to find a space on the first floor. On State Street, the last of the night's revelers still partied on, refusing to believe that the party was over. The barricades had been removed, the extra lights had been turned off; the street was pretty much empty. Phil headed down State.

The shops were closed, the bars were closed. But Phil intended to search each one for himself. It is what Edie would do, he told himself. He lengthened his stride and with that look of determination, he was let into each bar, even though they were closing.

At State and Gorham, he saw Gracie on the other side. They met in the middle of the street. What the hell, there wasn't any traffic.

"Why are you here?" demanded Gracie.

"Same reason you are," said Phil.

"No calls came into the department from her. I've checked," said Gracie. "Detox and hospitals are busy, but they didn't have any Edie Swifts or Jane Does when I called around."

"So, what are you thinking?"

"Nothing."

"What are you guessing?"

"Nothing."

"Any thought processes going on in your head?" yelled Phil.

"I'm thinking you should go home. Leave this to the police."

"No way," said Phil and started up State.

"Where you going?"

"To find Edie."

"Leave it for the police, go home."

Phil kept going. "The police can come, too."

"And where are you going to start looking?"

"Where every dirty dog goes . . . back to its home."

Gracie Davis watched Phil increase his stride. She ran to join him. "I'm coming."

"Got your gun?"

"Always," said Gracie as she broke into a jog to keep up with Phil.

35

*

They took Gracie's car. But, at his insistence, they stopped at Phil's.

He pulled his .30–06 from the trunk.

"Is that thing loaded?" quizzed Gracie.

"No. I know how to be a responsible hunter. The bullets are all in my pocket," said Phil. "We're burning daylight. Let's get this thing moving."

Gracie was intelligent. She didn't point out to Phil that it was night. She didn't want to push the buttons of a man on the edge.

They cruised out of the Doty Street ramp and onto the quiet dark streets of Madison.

"Can't you go any faster?" demanded Phil as they reached the edge of the suburbs that once upon a time had distinct borders with Madison.

"I'm going seventy."

"Not fast enough. Put your lights and sirens on. Do something!"

"We are doing something. We're speeding to the last known gathering place of an unknown entity—possibly a gang. I'm not using lights and sirens because I don't want to scare them away, if they are at Indian Lake."

"Where else would they be?"

"Depends on what their habits are." Gracie looked at Phil, who was pushing on the dash as if that would make the car go faster.

"Why are you taking this so lightly?" Phil yelled.

"I'm not. One of my best people has gone missing. I'm out in the middle of the night looking for her, not assigning that task to someone else. The best thing for us is to take a deep breath and a step back to see what we got. We need to keep our brains open."

"And what am I supposed to do, sing *Kumbaya*?"

"Yes, if that helps you. We don't know if Edie is in trouble. We don't know where she is. We don't know anything. The only thing we have now is our brains, and if we lose control of that, we're done for. So, I suggest you take a deep breath . . . NOW."

Phil took a deep breath.

"And sing *Kumbaya*."

"Don't know it," said Phil.

They were silent the rest of the way to Indian Lake.

Gracie drove around the park. Acres of corn still circled the park, where corn stubble stood nothing was visible from the road. "Damn those farmers, why hasn't this corn been harvested? Someone needs to light a fire under them," said Gracie.

Phil thought she was the person to do it.

Gracie parked near the entrance to Indian Lake Park.

"If they're here, there's no need to scare them into doing something we'll regret," Gracie said, checking that her first magazine was full and in place, and the second, and the third. She flicked her gun's safety off. Radio was on, sound low. Her cell had reception, she put it on vibrate. She looked over to Phil as he loaded his rifle. "Is that thing on safety?"

"No. Is yours?"

"No. But I know what I'm doing, I've used it before. I don't know about you. Put the safety on."

Phil complied. He told himself that it was only because she held a loaded gun.

They started for the hill.

Gracie grabbed Phil's arm when she caught up to him and whispered in his ear, "Slow down, stay together." The moon was full; Gracie saw anxiety and determination in Phil's face fighting for dominance. Best to keep any communication short and simple. "Follow my lead. My instructions. Understand?" She didn't let him go until he nodded yes.

Lieutenant Grace Davis led the way.

36

✳

At the top of the hill, Gracie stopped. She took a deep breath. A fire. She motioned to Phil to be quiet and started carefully down the path that she had explored with Edie only a few weeks before.

Halfway down the hill, Gracie and Phil halted. There, in the clearing, was a small fire. Some people gathered round it.

Gracie and Phil quickly settled in to wait for their eyes to adjust.

They could make out two people around the campfire. No, a third one joined them from the shadows.

Gracie and Phil watched as the third person stepped out of the circle of light cast by the fire, and then rejoined them a few seconds later.

Phil, putting his mouth near Gracie's ear, cupped his hands around it. "Recognize any of them?"

She shook her head.

They watched the third person as he walked in and out of the darkness surrounding the campfire. The two boys squatted near the fire, their heads down, and their backs to the man. As their eyes adjusted, Gracie and Phil could make out something on the ground at the edge of the woods.

Phil gasped.

Gracie shoved his face into the ground. "Shut up, fool," she whispered in his ear as she held his face in the ground for a few seconds before letting him up. Gracie put her face into his. "Maybe it is, maybe it isn't Edie. We wait. And you shut up."

Moments later, three people emerged from the woods to join the circle around the fire. The boys at the fire stood up.

Gracie leaned toward Phil. "One of the new boys is Ian Boehnen."

"You're late, Ian," Devin said.

"Sorry, Devin, had to wait for my parents to fall asleep and Eric to pick me up in his Jeep."

"What's wrong with your car?"

"It's up on hoists, my father decided to fix it tonight."

"See you brought the treat, like I told you," said Devin.

"What treat? We brought the girl," said Ian.

The girl lowered the hood of her sweatshirt.

"Boys, this one's for you. She wants to be part of our group. So, when we're done here, she's agreed to give each of you a treat," Devin said.

The boys around the fire stared at each other.

"Never had pussy before, Sean?" asked Eric Theis. "How about you Ted? Devin, it looks like all kinds of initiations are happening here tonight."

Ted picked up a handful of dirt and flung it at Eric. It took only a few steps for Eric to reach Ted, but Sean put his foot in Eric's way, sending Eric sprawling. A few quick body twists kept Eric out of the fire. Eric flipped over, grabbed Sean's leg and pulled him down. The two boys punched, kicked, bit as they rolled together on the ground. The flowing blood soon caked the dirt on their face.

Ted eyed the girl.

Devin watched as the boys beat on each other.

It was Ian who finally pulled the boys apart.

Sean and Eric sat on opposite sides of the fire; when they were able, they lifted their heads to glare at each other.

"You don't have to worry, Eric. Your family is friends with the governor. And they got money," Sean said.

"Like that ever did me any good," Eric said.

"Look at the car you drive," Ian said.

Eric put his head down on his knees again.

Ted bent over Eric. "I get the girl first."

"Don't want any sloppy seconds?" Eric asked.

The boys went silent, slipping into their own worlds.

"What you got over there?" asked the girl.

"Our latest victim," said Devin.

Eric glanced toward the shadows. With effort, he pushed himself off the ground and walked to where the bundle was curled.. "Hey, that's the bitchy cop who's been bothering my parents." He kicked her in the back. A groan came from the bundle. The second time, the kick was harder. The groan was louder.

Ian went to look at the bundle. "That's a cop. This is serious stuff. Should we be doing this? Aren't we in a shitload of trouble already?"

"The boss says not to worry, there's a new sheriff in town. I'm told the last one we took care of was from the FBI," said Devin. "It can't get worse than that."

"But we didn't know he was an FBI agent. You told us he dissed you, that he needed to be taught a lesson," said Sean.

"What lesson did an FBI guy have to learn?" Ian asked.

"Not to disrespect me. When I cleared his table, he stared right through me. I was shit to him. Later, I was walking past him and he shoved me into a building. It was brick and I still have the shoulder scabs to prove it. I should've taken him down then, but those State Street commies would've jumped me. And we taught him a lesson. We are in this together. We are a gang. And we will be respected," Devin said.

Ian and Sean looked at each other, shrugged their shoulders, but did not interrupt Devin's rants. Ian looked at the ground. Sean stared into the fire. Eric kept his eyes glued to Devin. Ted glanced from Eric to Devin and back again.

And I noticed you weren't pulling your weight then," said Devin. "If you're not part of this group, YOU will be next. Go give her a good kick."

Sean walked over to the bundle and placed a kick to her ass. Better her than him. He'd watched Devin drop into madness and stomp the FBI guy until the frenzy left his eyes.

Devin didn't have to say anything to Ted; he, too, walked to the bundle and kicked it.

The bundle moaned.

Devin went to check.

Devin knelt in front of Edie, grabbed her face. Her eyes weren't staring anymore. Edie was looking around.

"It's wearing off," said Devin. He grabbed his balls and pulled them up. "Maybe I should show the boys how it's done. Teach you a few things besides. Like putting you back where you belong," he said. He punched Edie's face and let it drop to the dirt. He went back to the fire and his boys. Their backs were turned to the fire. He stretched his hands toward the fire. "Not going to freeze these hands over that uppity bitch. We'll take our time and get it right, this time." Devin waited until the boys finished warming their butts and they turned to face the fire. "The boss is pleased with you. He wants us to move on and up."

"Who's this boss you keep referring to?" asked Eric.

"He knows your names, you don't need to know his," said Devin.

"When will I get to know it?" Eric was unwilling to drop the question.

"When it is time," replied Devin.

"When will that be?"

"When I'm told," said Devin.

Eric turned his back to the fire. He watched the bundle move. He didn't say anything.

Gracie placed her mouth next to Phil's ear, "I'm calling for assistance. Don't do anything. Understand?"

Phil nodded.

Gracie decided he could keep his rifle while she was away.

She slipped back up the hill to make her calls.

Phil lowered his head. He couldn't watch, and do nothing.

Even with his hands covering his ears, he heard Edie's moans when a kick or a fist landed. He wondered, even then, why he didn't jump up and blast each of those mealy-mouthed bastards in the face.

Gracie placed a hand on Phil's shoulder to let him know she was back. "Called for backup and an ambulance," she whispered. "Lights and sirens."

The bundle managed to inch toward the fire. Gracie and Phil could now see Edie's face. And the pain.

The girl walked over to Edie, studied her face, "Hey, I think I've seen this bitch before." The girl aimed a kick to Edie's chest. "Where have I seen her?" She squatted down to look closely at Edie. "She was the one in the store. She's the one who called the cops on us!" The girl stood and kicked Edie again. "Do you know what you did? I got jailed. I got a record now. My mother never wants to see me. And you're just like her, I bet." The girl kicked at Edie, again, but this time she missed.

"I can't take it anymore," said Gracie. She stood up. "This is the police. Stay where you are."

Devin ran for the woods.

The boys looked at each other.

Gracie began to shoot, reminding herself and Phil to fire over their heads.

The girl aimed a kick at Edie's guts.

Edie grabbed the foot, twisted it, and held on. She could never remember how.

The boys scattered.

The police sirens were surrounding the park.

Gracie shoved Phil into the front of the ambulance.

"Why aren't they moving?" Phil screamed.

"They're establishing an IV line, taking vitals, talking with the hospital."

"Can't they go faster? We gotta get her out of here, now."

"Let them do their job," said Gracie.

An EMT called from the back, "Lights and sirens."

"Gotta go, Lieutenant," said the driver, looking at Gracie.

"She'll be fine," said Gracie as she slammed the door. She watched as the ambulance pulled away and hoped that what she said was true.

37

*

Phil sat alone in the surgery waiting room, his head in his hands. He didn't notice that the lights were low. Or that blankets and pillows were on a cart beside the door. Or that there were a few snacks still left at the desk for the off-hours emergency surgeries. Phil didn't see anything.

He didn't see Gracie throw a blanket around his shoulders. He didn't see Aunt Jill sit beside him or feel her holding his hand.

Morning brought inconsiderate, noisy people to the surgical waiting room who turned on the damned TV, or who talked on their cells, telling the world their secrets. Phil pulled the blanket tighter, then saw that an official-looking person was sitting at the reception desk.

"Excuse me," said Phil, standing in front of the desk, holding the blanket tight around him.

"What can I do for you?" asked the receptionist.

"Is Edie Swift still in surgery?"

"Let me check. How do you spell the last name?"

"S–W–I–F–T."

The receptionist typed the name into the computer. "Sorry, there's no one by that name in surgery. There is an Edith Swift in the surgical ICU."

"Where's that?"

"Go out of this room, take the elevators to your left to fifth floor, and follow the signs."

Phil turned to leave.

"Maybe you should put the blanket in the hamper by the door," said the receptionist.

Phil looked down. He was clutching a blanket. He didn't know how it got there. He took it off, threw it into the hamper, turned left, and rode the elevator to the fifth floor.

Outside the double doors to the surgical ICU sat a receptionist, a sweet young thing. Phil walked past her, pushed against the doors. They didn't budge.

"Excuse me, sir, may I help you?" asked the receptionist.

"I'd like to see Edie Swift."

"Are you family?"

"Not exactly."

"I'm sorry, but the policy states that I can only admit family."

"How am I supposed to see her?"

"You can call her surgeon and get permission."

"What's his name?"

"That's confidential." The ICU receptionist looked at her notes. "There is someone with her now."

"Can you give me a name?"

"I'm sorry, that's confidential."

"Then how can I call?"

"I'm sorry, we don't allow cell phones in the ICU."

The receptionist's face brightened, "Are you on the list?"

"What list?"

"The list of people to whom we may release the patient's information."

"I'm Phil Best."

The receptionist looked him up on the computer.

"Sorry, sir, you are not on the list."

"But—" Phil started to say.

"He's with me," said Gracie as she grabbed Phil's arm on her way to the locked doors. She was buzzed in, dragging Phil with her in her wake.

Lieutenant Grace Davis wasn't going to take shit from anyone that day. Last night hadn't gone well. And this day was following suit. Starting with one of her deputies at the hospital, fighting for her life.

She'd led off at shift report. Most of the deputies had heard bits and pieces about last night, and they wanted to know the whole story. But when they entered the report room chattering to each other they saw Lieutenant Davis and quietly, and quickly, took a seat, if they could find one. The room was packed. It was standing–room only. The day shift took what seats the night shift left empty, and the rest filled in the spaces against the walls. The latecomers had to be satisfied with standing in the hallway and only hearing half of the report. They'd be clued in later. And somehow they all knew that Lieutenant Grace Davis was pissed. Mugshots of the juveniles, the young woman and the photos, courtesy of Jerome Adler, of Devin Miller, aka Devin King, and other possible aliases, could be seen on the wall.

Gracie started with a warning that there was a blackout on this case. She warned her deputies that there would be no pillow talk, no leaks. If anything leaked, she was coming for the deputy that leaked the information.

As her report went on, the tension in the room grew. By the time she left, everyone was out for bear. Gracie left Fred Price to finish the report, but as she left the room she turned toward the sound of crying. In a corner she saw Ben Harris step in front of Sadie Carpenter to shield her from the other deputies. She didn't care, her concern was for Edith Swift.

Edie's room was across from the nurses' station. The curtains were pulled, but the door was open. Aunt Jill was sitting by Edie's bed.

"Phil, you look like hell," said Aunt Jill, rising from the chair to hug him. "Sorry I didn't wake you, thought you needed to sleep."

Phil took Jill's seat beside Edie's bed. He covered Edie's hand with his. He took in everything that was hooked to Edie: there was an IV line in each arm, things that were wrapped around her legs that were inflating and deflating, a catheter that was draining her bladder, a breathing tube forcing air into her lungs, a tube that came out of her nose to drain dark stuff from her stomach, a tube that come out of her abdomen, leads that went from her chest to a monitor. He looked at the monitor; he didn't understand anything that was displayed. He looked back at Edie. She was still. He'd never seen her so still. He'd always known Edie as a bundle of energy. Phil knew that Edie would not have liked all these contraptions, but he didn't care—they were keeping his love alive.

"She came through surgery okay," said Aunt Jill. "They took a kidney, part of her large intestine, and . . . and . . . and they have her in an induced coma." Aunt Jill took a deep breath, let it out slowly, the surgeon could tell Phil the rest. "A nurse tells me that one of those bags is for fluid, another for pain meds, another for antibiotics, another for blood pressure, and another for food." Aunt Jill struggled to keep from breaking down. "The surgeon would like her to rest for now. Who's with Hillary?"

"A neighbor."

"I'll go out and get her. Does your family know?"

"No."

"I'll call your mother. She can tell everyone else."

"You do that," said Phil, looking at Edie.

Aunt Jill came back late in the afternoon. Phil hadn't moved.

"Go home, Phil, your daughter needs you."

"I can't leave Edie alone."

"I'll be here."

"They won't let me back in."

"I put you on the list."

"Why you? Why not me?"

"It's a screwy system. Go home. Hillary needs you. Eat, your kitchen is filling up with food. Come back tomorrow morning after you've slept, showered, changed clothes, and eaten."

Aunt Jill kissed Edie's pale cheek, brushed stray hairs from Edie's forehead, then sat in the still warm chair that Phil had vacated. She took Edie's hand in hers, it was cool. "Edie, I hope you can hear me, they say that is the last thing that goes. Edie, don't leave us. I'll raise your baby, if I have to. Just like I raised you. But I'd rather be on the sidelines watching you raise her and helping when you need me. Edie, stay."

38

✳

Lieutenant Davis led off the morning shift report: no changes in Edie Swift's condition. "The four boys . . ." Gracie started.

"They're not boys anymore," someone shouted from the back of the room.

"The four young men have gone quiet, no one is talking. The D.A.'s office is still reviewing the reports and considering all possible charges. They will be charged in adult court," said Gracie.

"'Bout time," someone shouted.

"The Feds are looking at charges of their own. The Feds and our D.A. will be working out who has priority. The young woman is talking," Gracie continued.

"Rumor has it that she's crying for her mama," a third voice added.

Gracie had enough, "I understand the anger in this room, I didn't think that I needed to remind you that we are here to serve and protect the public. None of what I am hearing in this room reflects our standards. Your anger stays in this room. If anyone needs to talk, call someone on the Peer Support Team, your sergeant, me.

We will schedule a debriefing, if needed. We end this jibberish, here and now. Am I understood?"

A murmur of assent swept through the room.

"And, furthermore, what I want is to get the bastard that got away." What Gracie wanted, she usually got.

The next morning Edie's condition had not changed. Phil replaced Aunt Jill in the bedside vigil.

That night when Phil left the hospital he saw a TV crew filming outside the entrance. He stepped back into the hospital and wandered until he found a back door. He was in no mood to be the lead story on the evening news. All he wanted was for everyone to leave him and his family alone.

39

*

Lieutenant Davis had to report the next morning that nothing had changed. Edith Swift was still in critical condition. The D.A.'s office was carefully considering the charges to be brought against the boys; they expected a preliminary hearing tomorrow. Groans went through the room when a deputy shouted that he had heard that one of the boys had political connections—high up.

Nothing had changed at the hospital that day, at least not that Phil could see. Edie was still hooked up to lots of IVs, still had a catheter which still had blood dripping along with the urine, still had those inflatable sequential compression devices, SCDs to anyone working the hospital floor, on her legs, he had been here too long, he was learning the acronyms of the hospital. And she did not move. But he learned from the doctors that Edie's blood pressure was rising. They didn't like that. What they didn't like, Phil didn't like.

40

*

The next day Lieutenant Davis had no new updates on Edith Swift, or her case. She was getting seriously ticked off. The deputies were too. They vowed to step up their game, they wanted the bastard.

That day Phil was tired. He was tired of hospital smells, tired of hospital food, tired of being told what to do, tired of his baby crying for her mother. So he brought his baby to the hospital.
He was buzzed into the ICU. But, outside Edie's room, he was stopped by a nurse.

"You take that baby out of here. This is no place for her."
"Fuck off," said Phil and took his Hillary into the room to be reunited with her mother.
Phil gently arranged a nest for Hillary in her mother's arm, and then settled into his chair beside Edie's bed to monitor mother and child.

Moments later the nurse rushed into the room, whisked Hillary back into Phil's arms and checked each line, from source to the end, and then back again. Then checked all lines a second time. She quickly left the room. Phil heard her call to Edie's surgeon. And over the P.A. system, heard the surgeon called to the ICU. Phil wondered what it was about, but he didn't care, he'd find out, soon. Again, he made a nest in Edie's arms for Hillary. When he was done he looked up to see her surgeon standing in the doorway staring at the monitor.

"Her blood pressure is down, her heart rate has dropped to within a normal range, and her breathing rate is also within normal," is all the doctor said before he left.

Later that day Aunt Jill persuaded Phil to take Hillary home.

Phil didn't notice the TV crew outside the hospital when he left. But Mark Uselman noticed Phil. Leigh Stone did not.

"This is Leigh Stone reporting. The sheriff's department has yet to release the name of the deputy injured Saturday night at Indian Lake Park. They are waiting for all family members to be notified. The hospital reports that the deputy is in serious but stable condition. A source that has asked not to be identified states that the deputy is . . ."

Mark Uselman stepped in front of the camera and took the mike away from Leigh Stone. "No more. You are putting yourself and your station at risk. Let me give you a lesson in responsible journalism—"

"From you?"

Mark ignored the comment. "This is a relatively small market. So, in some new stories, if we want to keep our sources, we report the facts as given from official sources. This is one of those times. Everything else with this case is rumor. We investigate those rumors, we don't report them. We don't report them until we've got confirmation from a different reliable source that they aren't rumor. You should have learned that in journalism school. Most of all, we protect our sources."

Leigh Stone's temper flared. "What I learned in school was to get the story and get it first. The buzz is that it is her. I'll take the flak. Now get out of my way. I've got a story to report."

"Keep gossip out of it."

"The source is reliable."

"Have you confirmed that with a second reliable source?"

"No. No one is talking."

"Then your first source should be willing to be named by you. If not, I haven't filed my report yet . . . and I will name the source and you. I know who it is, we use the same one."

Leigh glared at Mark. A moment later he stepped away from the camera, he noticed that Phil and child were across the street and down the block. But he stayed to watch the report.

"Let's take it from the top," Leigh said to her cameraman. "This is Leigh Stone reporting. The police are still waiting for family members to be notified before releasing the name of the deputy injured at Indian Lake Saturday night. A hospital spokesman said that the deputy's condition is serious but stable. The district attorney's office states they are reviewing this case to determine the appropriate charges for the four juvenile males in custody who will be waived into adult court. The female alleged to have taken part in the assault is an adult and will be charged in adult court. The police are still searching for a fifth person who was involved: Devin Miller, alias Devin King, is thought to have left the area."

Making certain that the camera was turned off, Mark asked Leigh, "Is this the end of the story?"

"Probably," said Leigh. "No one is talking . . . officially."

"For now, I'm calling it a wrap. You lose. I think Friday night at the Ovens with the gang will be fine. See you at seven?"

"I'll send my credit card."

"It wouldn't be the same. We'd rather have you and your credit card, in person.

41

✴

The next day, by the time Phil got to the hospital, the ventilator had been removed, replaced with a nasal cannula, but multiple lines still went into and out of Edie. But Phil could kiss her, and possibly, maybe, talk to her and she could whisper back to him.

"Marry me," Phil asked.

"Why?" Edie whispered.

"I want to take care of you."

"I'm not your little woman," said Edie and closed her eyes.

Phil kept her hand in his, turned on the TV, and let it drone on in the background. The nurses said it was okay.

42

✳

A week later, Edie was still in the hospital.

Phil, more relaxed in his vigil, said, "Marry me."

"Why?"

"Because they needed Aunt Jill's permission to do surgery. They didn't ask me. They asked Aunt Jill. We live together. We have a child together. But they called Aunt Jill. Not me."

"Aunt Jill raised me. She knows a lot," said Edie.

"I know a lot. We have long pillow talks and other sweet things. We have learned each other's needs, wants, hopes for the future. But I was shoved to the side. Aunt Jill directed your life when you couldn't. Not me."

"It was an emergency."

"She is not the one who keeps you warm at night. She is not the one who watches you walk out the door each morning and wonders if you will be coming back or if she'll be attending your funeral. I am. When I moved in with you, it wasn't just for the pleasure of your company. I want it all. The good and the bad."

"I can make you my health care power of attorney."

"I want more. I want to marry you. I want your days and my days to be wrapped around each other. And no one able to question that."

"There's that possession thing, again."

"Damn it, Edie. I will be yours, you will be mine. I love you."

"What about your mother?"

"This is between you and me. Marry me. I love you."

Edie was silent.

Phil looked to see if she was awake.

"We'll see," said Edith Swift as she fell asleep with her hand in his.

About the Author

Julia Hoffman lives in Wisconsin with her family. She is working on the next Edie Swift story.

89606295R10154

Made in the USA
Lexington, KY
01 June 2018